MARKED

BY CAPONE

Life Changing Books *in conjunction with* Power Play Media
Published by Life Changing Books
P.O. Box 423 Brandywine, MD 20613

Library of Congress Cataloging-in-Publication Data;

www.lifechangingbooks.net

13 Digit: 978-1934230885
10 Digit: 1-934230885

ACKNOWLEDGEMENTS

How do you thank so many people that have had some kind of impact on your life? I'm sure there will be someone that gets left out by name, but just know this, it's not intentional. Charge it to my head, and not my heart.

First and foremost I want, need, and have to thank and give all of the glory to you God. Without the sacrifice that He made many thousands of years ago, there would be no me. I want to thank my mother, Mechelle Glenn and my father Curtis Glenn for your continued love, support, and prayers. I often wonder how I got so lucky to have a mom and pop like the two of you. I'm still going to need the both of you to back away from the kitchen though. LOL

Thank you to my wonderful and beautiful wife, Reco. When I didn't think I could, you said I can. When I said I didn't know if I could be good at it, you said I already was. When I said I don't feel like it, you said I need to. Thank you for supporting and believing in me. I also gotta thank you for your patience for all the times I was burning the road up before I ever got signed.

To my wonderful, beautiful and inspiring baby girls, Aure, Deja, Kianna, and Jasmine. Daddy loves the four of you more than any amount of words can express. Thank you for your unconditional love. There are so many times when I think that I'm so undeserving of all the love that you all give me. You all continually teach me what it means to have an agape kind of love. I'm so very proud of each and every one of you.

I want to thank you Auntie Rusty for always being there for me and having my back when I needed it the most. We've been like Burt and Ernie, Ren and Stimpy, Batman and Robin, and Bonnie and Clyde from day one.

Big Ma, Grandma Sharon and Granny, I love the three of you more than anything I could ever say. Auntie Lisa and Granddaddy Tom, you have been an inspiration to me for so many years now. You are the definition of courage.

Uncle Nate, thank you for showing me what it is to be a real G. I've been pissed off as hell since the day you got sent up state to do time behind a bunch of BS. Don't worry though, your feet will touch down soon enough, and when you do, we gon' get this money together. Uncle Von, man how can I thank you and apologize to you at the same time? You showed me what real pimpin' and g-ridin really was about. Thank you for all the times when you held me down when I needed some food or money.

To my brother and sister, TeAndre and Mya. Everyday I'm thankful that before our pops was killed, he left me with the two of you. I wish I could turn back the hands of time and make it so the three of us would've never been apart. I love you guys more than anything and whenever you need your big brother you just let me know. I'll come with them thangs blazin'.

To my surrogate brothers, Robert "Jack" Jackson, Dennis "Denny Den" Lee, and Willie "Peanut" Gage. Jack, thanks for always being the voice of reason when I needed to hear it. I may not have always liked it, but I can't deny you've always been right. Denny Den, you are the epitome of what big brother is supposed to be. I can't remember the last time I ever needed or wanted something when I was around you. Thank you for always having my back, whether I was wrong or right.

Meka and Dee Dee, I am so lucky to have a sisters like you. Both of you are crazy as all out doors. Meka thank you for taking such good care of Aure for me when I was in the Marines. To my nieces Essence, Shamiqua, and Kenitria, and my nephew Bobo, I love you guys. Britt-Britt, since day one you have been more like a little sister to me than a cousin. Know this, you mean the world to me, there is NOTHING that I wouldn't do for Brittney G. Lee. I love you.

Momma and Thomas, thank you for all the support and love that you guys have given me over the years. Thank you for never making me feel like anything other than a member of the immediate family. Big Butch, thank you for always being so thoughtful and loving toward me. Lil Butch, you are exactly what a brother-in-law should be. I can't wait for you to come back around this way. Ms. Steph, thank you for always showing your brother-in-law so much love.

I gotta thank my mother and father in Christ, Bishop Frank and Pastor JoeNell Summerfield. Your teachings are not only life changing, but revelational as well. I love the both of you to life. Frank Jr., Mitch, Valisha, and Joshua thank you for sharing your family with me. James, Dominique, and baby Jacquline, thank you for allowing me and my family to be a part of your lives.

Now, to my LCB family. Man, how can I thank you guys for taking a chance on me? Azarel, thank you so much for everything. There are so many times that I think I'm so undeserving of being on your team, but you always make me feel like a part of the family. When I look at you, I see the essence of what a go getter is and should be. I'm so lucky to have someone like you in my corner.

Leslie "Pitbull In A Skirt" Allen, WOW... how do I thank you? How do you tell someone that you admire them yet fear them at the same time? LOL... I guess I just did. I can't possibly thank you enough for all that you do and have done for me. When I was going through one of the most difficult times in my life you didn't give up on me or Marked, and I thank you for that. We are so lucky to have you. One day I'll figure out how to properly thank you and Azarel. Until then, know that I'm so very appreciative, and indebted to both of you. Thank you for believing in me and this project. I love you both dearly!!!

Tonya Ridley, you are another one that I can't find the right words for. I can't thank you enough for EVERYTHING that you do and have done for not just me, but for Reco and Jas too. Thank you for being our grocery store, babysitter, cab, and supporter. From the first time I met you, you never treated me like an outsider. Honestly, had it not been for you, I wouldn't be anything close to an author. Thanks for believing in me. I love you, Josh, and Jackie tremendously.

To my brother and sister authors on the LCB roster, I just wanted to let you all know, in the words of DJ Khaled, "WE TAKIN' OVER!" Also to the world's greatest publicist, Nakea

Murray. Thank you for all that you've done to make this project a success.

To my best friends on the planet, Bobo, Trice and my God-Daughters Briaa and Brandyn, Sticky, Ray, Steve and Dre. Y'all niggas keep a nigga grounded. Thank you. Ju, Nate, Butter, Shay and Snook, Erika and baby Chris, Shae, Diaja, Mikayla, Coco and Lil Dave I love you. Duck, Ken, Meka-Lee, Taz, Black, D-Bo, Mee Mee, Kee Kee, Dupree, and Victoria. Sean and Tiffany Simmons, Chris Lewis, Howard Toomer, Keith and Samantha Barnhill, thanks for showing a nigga new ways to get money! Lil Randy, Robin, Kendra, and the rest of my cousins, I love you all to life. To my work friends Burton, Rome, Clif, Davis, Self, Wes, Scott, Walt, Thomas, Michele, Christina, Rebecca, Leanna, Fatima, Efrem, Duane, Maurice, and Kareem, thank you!!! To Lynn, Kiera, Buddy and and my God-Son Cahner, I love you all. J'Ton and your great book club Women of Essence, thank you. To my arch-nemesis Sadie and your off the chain sister Taylor, I love you both dearly. Jackie Davis and Poobie, I can't to see the two of you blow up. Karen "Always Looking Out The Window" Hodges, you know I couldn't leave you and Danny out of the thank you's. Empire Records and Most Wanted Crown Holders Records thanks for holding me down. To the realest nigga in all of music, Petey Pablo, keep doing your thang my dude.

Now, to the part that means the most to me, but also hurts the most. I'm a son that lost his father and a father that lost his son. RIP to my father, Thomas Allan Pride, my son Rashaan Arnez Mc-Carver, my cousins Randy Lamar Bush, Jonetta "JoJo" Moore, Thee-Baby, my Pastor Laverne Joyce, my granddaddy's Ray Mc-Carver and Nat-Coolie Simpson, my grandma Verne Pride, my greatgrandma Nanny, to the coolest dude I've ever met, Michael Ridley, and all the other family and friends that I've lost over the years. I miss you all and still think of every last one of you every-day. Pontiac, Detroit, Raleigh, and everywhere I've ever rested my head, I love you. Like I said in the beginning, if I left your name out it was not intentional, charge it to my head and not my heart.

CAPONE

CHAPTER 1

Blaring from behind, Deluxe didn't notice the screaming police siren when he and his uncle Gator, coasted down Jefferson Avenue. *'Duffle Bag Boy'* by Playaz Circle and Lil' Wayne, blasted through the Bose speaker system that Gator had just installed into his customized, money green, 2007 Mercedes CLS500.

"Damn, it's 'bout to be a long night Nephew," Gator said, to Deluxe before turning the music down. "This 4th of July gonna be some shit to remember."

"Why? What's up?"

"Look in yo' side view mirror. The fuckin' cops behind us."

Deluxe pushed aside any concern as he looked in the mirror. "We should be straight. You still got yo' car registered in yo' girl's name right? So ain't shit to worry about Unc," Deluxe told him nonchalantly. He looked over at his uncle with a grin on his chiseled face. However, the next few words he heard fucked up any positive thoughts he once had.

"Fuck whatever name the car is in nigga. I got twenty-five

of them thangs in the trunk."

Feeling as if his life, career, and freedom were coming to a fast end, Deluxe began to shake his head back and forth. *How did I end up in this fucked up situation? Why does Unc have twenty-five kilos of coke in the trunk anyway? Why ain't Myth carrying this shit?* Deluxe thought as he tried to put the pieces to the puzzle together.

Looking through the rearview mirror, Gator could see the tall lanky officer in street clothes walking toward them with an arrogant swagger. Approaching the driver side window like he was the shit, the officer stood with an evil smirk on his dark face as Gator hit the button for the automatic window. Cigarette smoke oozed from the officer's wide nostrils into the car. The smell of his Newport immediately destroyed the piña colada scent that once filled the car.

"Gimmie your fucking license and registration," the cop demanded in a deep, arrogant voice. Waiting on a response, he pointed a bright flash light around the car stopping dead on Deluxe's face.

"Well, well, well, if it isn't Detective Punk-Ass Hughes," Gator replied. He pulled out his license, and then reached for the glove compartment to retrieve the registration. "Haven't you learned yo' lesson already about fuckin' wit' me muthafucka? Why in the hell did you pull me over?"

Deluxe's eyes grew two times their normal size. He couldn't believe the way his uncle was talking to the detective. In his mind, he knew some shit was about to go down.

Hughes flicked his cigarette to the ground. "You better watch your fucking mouth, Mr. Gerald Green. I pulled you over because your ass didn't come to a complete stop at that stop sign back there. Now gimmie your damn license and registration," the detective ordered, snatching the items from Gator's grip.

"Complete stop my ass. Y'all pussy- ass cops can't stand to see a nigga eatin'. Broke- ass muthafuckas," Gator taunted in a confrontational voice.

Hughes displayed one of those shit eating grins that crooked-ass cops from the Detroit Police Department normally had. "You real fucking proud of that drug money you make, huh? Well, your ass won't be eating for long," he said. He turned, then walked back to his car like a true asshole.

"Unc, are you crazy? Deluxe asked. "Why you startin' shit, knowin' what's in the trunk?"

"Fuck that nigga. He been tryin' to lock me up for years."

Ever since Gator had beaten his first drug case, a conspiracy charge back in 1995, Detective Hughes had it in for Gator's entire drug operation. It was Hughes first year on the Narcotics

Task Force when he and Gator went head to head. Detective Hughes thought that he had an open and shut case against Gator until the state's star witness, Tommy Young, aka Young Bird was found floating face down in the Detroit River with his tongue cut out and two bullets in the back of his head.

Everyone in the city of Detroit was present for the trial to see what the outcome would be, especially all the other hustlers, who were already trying to take over Gator's territory. One side of the court room was filled with all of the people who thought that Gator should go away for life, especially for spreading what they called poison in the community. The other side was full of his biggest supporters, including his long time girlfriend Mylani, his mother Momma Ruth, and his entire crew, who were all ready to set things off at the wink of his eye.

With his Jewish lawyers by his side, Gator stood in a custom made three button Versace suit, along with his signature alligator shoes as the judge read the jury's verdict. The court room erupted with sighs, laughter and tears as the charge of conspiracy to deliver more than six hundred and fifty grams of a controlled substance came back with a not guilty verdict.

Hearing the judge pound his gavel declared victory as Gator shook his attorney's hand, revealing his gaudy four carat diamond bracelet with the matching pinky ring. He winked and laughed at Hughes as he walked out of the court room a free man. After being embarrassed, Hughes made a vow to get Gator and anyone involved with his criminal enterprise off the streets for good, even if that meant committing murder. Thirteen years later, he was still trying.

"Listen, I need you to handle this nigga for me," Gator whispered to Deluxe.

"Don't you still have Hatchett & Steinberg on the books? Call those shady muthafuckin' lawyers and have 'em file a harassment complaint on Hughes. Shit that's what you payin' 'em for."

"Nigga look!" Gator exclaimed in a stern voice. "This is serious. If he decides to call the dogs out, it's gonna be a fuckin' rap. A possession and traffickin' charge wit' twenty five keys is gonna be damn near impossible to beat. Now I need you to put in work like you did on my first case...you know like that Young Bird shit." Gator slowly reached for a black towel underneath the driver's seat.

The mention of Young Bird's name instantly made Deluxe lower his head. Over the years he'd tried to block out the thoughtless murder that he'd committed on the states witness during his uncle's murder trail. He was only fourteen at the time. Now, at twenty-six, he was more mature and realized he'd taken away someone's life.

Deluxe cleared his throat then looked at his uncle Gator, whose dark complexion was close to midnight. "I don't know Unc. I mean that shit was a long time ago. You know I been tryin' to change. Plus, I'll get kicked out the military if I do that."

Gator became furious. "Nigga did you fuckin' hear me? Ain't no way around this. I ain't never ask you to put in work for the fam since that shit went down, and now you wanna act like a bitch. I mean, you actin' like you don't know how to carry out a job or somethin'. I was the first person to put a gat in yo' damn hands. Besides, since bein' in the Marines yo' ass should be like a fuckin' assassin or some shit by now." He looked at Deluxe sternly.

"Man, it's not even a question on whether I know how to shoot or not, but..." Deluxe tried to reply.

"But what, nigga? If you don't do this, all we gonna be doing is fightin' off faggots in the muthafuckin' penitentiary!"

Deluxe smiled. The last thing he was worried about was someone ever trying to fuck him without his consent. Reflecting on his uncle's words, Deluxe wanted to ask Gator, why he had to do the dirty work, but decided against it. He knew better than to ask a question like that. Questioning his uncle at a time like this would've been a sign of ultimate disrespect. After all, it was Gator who'd raised Deluxe since he was twelve; taught him how to be a man, and who'd also stepped up to fill the shoes of his father.

"I need you to step up and put one in this muthafucka's head," Gator said, causing Deluxe to come out of his daze. Gator unfolded the black towel, exposing a .45 semi-automatic handgun, then used the towel to place the gun in Deluxe's lap.

As Detective Hughes walked back toward the car, Deluxe's heart raced at the thought of possibly killing a cop. As a sniper in the Marines, killing people wasn't anything new to him, but a cop was un-chartered territory. The anticipation from what was about to go down caused the sweat from his back to soak the black Polo shirt he wore. Deluxe could hear his drill instructor Sgt. Jones screaming, *"One shot, one kill"* in his head over and over as Hughes inched closer to the car.

"It's do or die, nigga," Gator whispered, as he quickly laid his seat all the way back. He didn't want to be in the way when the bullets starting flying. "Handle this shit."

Preparing to enter the ranks of cop killer, Deluxe took a deep breath, and closed his eyes for a second. When Hughes appeared in front of the window, Deluxe quickly opened his eyes and aimed the gun in the detective's direction before pulling the trigger. The bullet instantly caught Hughes, six inches below the chin and into his throat. His aim was immaculate.

"See, that's what the fuck I'm talkin' 'bout!" Gator shouted, as he quickly sat up. Just in time to see Hughes' body collapse to the ground. "Damn Nephew, I guess that military shit did pay off."

A huge smile was planted on his face as he looked out the window at Hughes lifeless body. Gator quickly opened the door, jumping out to retrieve his license and registration that were lying on the ground. He also grabbed the detective's citation book, which he was certain held a ticket with all his information in it. He tried his best to get as much evidence as he could before getting back into the car. "Let's get the fuck out of here!"

Letting out one of the sickest laughs that Deluxe had ever heard, Gator sped off burning rubber in the process. The sight of Detective Hughes grabbing his throat and massive amounts of blood oozing through his hand began replaying in Deluxe's mind. As a Scout Sniper, Deluxe knew he would have to use his military training on the street one day, he just never thought it would be on a cop, no matter how dirty they were. Guilt sat in immediately. *Damn,* Deluxe thought to himself as they continued to their next destination.

Sounding like they were in the front row of a Biggie Smalls concert, '*Who Shot Ya,*' blasted through the speakers as Gator pulled up to the entrance of Belle Isle twenty minutes later. Deluxe could vaguely hear his uncle asking him, "You a'ight nigga? You lookin' a lil' squeamish and shit over there." Sounding like he was talking in slow motion, Deluxe then heard him say, "Look, I know it's been a long time since you had to take care of somebody, but trust me you'll get used to it."

However, that was just it. With the position that he was in, Deluxe only wanted to kill for his country. "It's not that easy."

Gator looked like he wanted to punch Deluxe in his mouth. "You need to man up right now. How is it that a fuckin' sniper in the Marines can kill them sand niggas with no problem, but then act like a bitch when it comes to puttin' in work out here on these streets!"

"It ain't like that," Deluxe replied in his defense.

"Well then, what the fuck are you cryin' about then? That bitch-ass cop got what he had comin' to him for a long time now. Shit, I couldn't have planned it any better."

What the fuck does that shit mean, Deluxe wondered as more thoughts began to race through his frazzled mind. "Do you think anyone saw us?" he asked, obviously still a little shaken from remembering the look on Hughes' face when the bullet hit him.

"This is the D nigga; muthafuckin' murda Motown. Aint no body sayin' shit even if they did see us. If niggas didn't speak up when Rock was killed or when you put in work wit' Young Bird, what makes you think someone gonna say somethin' now? We aint called the murder capital for nothin'." Gator smiled exposing his new, expensive set of porcelain veneers. Deluxe just glared at him remembering how his mouth used to remind him of a jack o' lantern on Halloween.

Gator was right, in a city like Detroit nobody ever talked to the police about anything that they saw going down. That was and always had been an unwritten law of the streets. It was these same kill or be killed streets of Detroit that had also taken the life of Deluxe's father, Ronald Green, or Rock as he was known around the hood. He earned the nickname when he and Gator got started in the game, for always having that "rock" on deck for the fiends. However, it was also the same streets that remained quiet when he was gunned down from a drug deal gone bad outside of Olympia's Coney Island on 7 Mile and Greenfield. Deluxe was left hoping that the streets would remain as quiet as they'd always been until he went back to his base in Cherry Point, North Carolina once his leave was up. But in a city where everyone was always looking for the next come up, anything could and most likely would happen.

CHAPTER 2

Belle Isle was the local hot spot where any and everybody went to get their floss on before hitting the streets for the night. As usual, the scene on the island was like a car show, from pimped out rides, loud music, to plenty of the cities baddest bitches, wearing little or nothing. The island had at all. Traffic was already out of control as Gator and Deluxe turned into the hot spot. It didn't take long to realize the line of custom painted Impala's sitting on vogues and daytons were the cars holding everybody up.

"Come on, get the fuck out the way!" Gator yelled as he pressed on his horn with rage. He dared anybody to respond to his impatience. He turned to Deluxe. "I hate these young muthafuckas, who think they doin' somethin' out here just cause they makin' a few dollars on the block. Little do they know, I run this mutha-fuckin' city, and most of the shit they sellin' come from me." He continued to vent while they passed more tricked out cars and the shiesty niggas from 7 Mile, who were making tons of noise.

"Where the hell is Myth's ass posted up at anyway?" Deluxe asked out loud.

Myth was Gator's best friend and right hand man of his drug empire. Myth, Gator and his brother Rock had grown up together in Jefferies projects on the west side of Detroit, one of the worst hoods in the city. Myth had just been released from a six year bid for a possession with the intent to deliver charge that he eventually beat on appeal. Gator held him down while he was away, keeping his commissary tight and making sure no off brand niggas tried to run up in his baby mamma, nor play daddy to his son while he was away. With that type of loyalty, it was easy to see why Myth felt like he owed Gator. As soon as he got out, Myth made sure he was partially responsible for increasing the families control and territory around the city, which didn't take long at all.

"See what happens when you on my payroll Nephew?" Gator asked, pulling up in front of Myth and his cousin Kane. Gator eyed the new black Lexus 460LS the two men were standing beside and smiled. "Yeah, wit' all the money we make, my nigga stays in somethin' tight."

Although Deluxe nodded and was in awe of the luxury vehicle that could parallel park itself, he still couldn't get the picture of Hughes out of his mind.

Gator didn't waste anytime jumping out of his car with

Deluxe not far behind. "What up doe, nigga?" he yelled walking up to Myth.

"Gangsta Gator, what up?" Myth replied. "What took y'all so long?"

Gator gave Myth some dap and the infamous what's up head nod to Myth's cousin Kane. He stared at the youngsta from New York coldly. "We had a small situation on the way over, no biggie though, cause Nephew here put in some serious work. That shit still got me goin'."

"Oh yeah? That nigga Deluxe finally steppin' up to the plate around this bitch, huh? It's about time. I know Rock would be proud as hell right about now. We always knew that military Rambo shit would benefit the fam one day." Myth looked at Deluxe and smiled, then gave him the infamous ghetto handshake.

Gator shook his head. "Shit, that nigga Rock would actually be pissed right now if he knew what I had his son doin'. You know his ass was always tryin' to keep Deluxe out the street when he was a kid. Think about it, Rock was mad when I gave him the nickname Deluxe. He actually wanted everybody to call him by his whack-ass real name, Jayson. Now what the fuck would I look like callin' his ass that shit? Ain't no gangstas named Jayson!"

Everybody laughed, including Deluxe.

"Yeah you right 'bout that shit. Rock would probably fuck

13

you up if he was livin' right now," Myth said. He opened the back door of his car and pulled out a white plastic bag from Mr. Alan's Shoes & Sportswear store, then closed the door gently. "Who was it that got sent to a early retirement anyway?" Myth asked Deluxe, while handing the plastic bag over to Gator. They used a bag from a different store every week for their transactions.

As Gator walked over to put the bag in his car, Deluxe looked over at Kane, who he'd never seen before. He was hesitant to talk around the unfamiliar man at first, but finally decided to speak up. He also tried to hide the fact that he was still a little fucked up about bodying a cop.

"You remember Detective Hughes, who's been dick ridin' y'all niggas for years?" Deluxe asked.

"No doubt I remember that faggot. He been tryin' to get somethin' on me and Gator for a minute now. That's how it is when niggas be gettin' all this bread. I remember he thought I was goin' away for a while when they got me on that bullshit posses-sion charge. I wish someone woulda bodied his ass a long time ago," Myth said. "So, what you doin' in town anyway solider?"

"I always take leave for the 4ᵗʰ of July. I'll be in the D for at least another week."

"Look like you the one settin' off the fireworks son," Kane finally replied, showing his cockiness.

Deluxe looked at Kane who'd been quiet the whole time and frowned. Kane's light complexion and bushy eyebrows reminded him of Al B. Sure, except for the long dread locks that crawled from under his New York Yankees hat. *Who the fuck is this nigga talking to*, he thought.

Myth could sense the uneasiness and decided to speak up. "Oh, Deluxe this is my cousin, Kane from New York. He been workin' for the family now for a minute."

"Yeah son, no disrespect on what I said. I was just complementin' yo' skills," Kane added, showing a set of gold teeth through his smile.

Just like Gator, Deluxe only replied with a head nod.

As Myth continued to fill Deluxe in about Kane's position, a black cherry Cadillac STS slowly crept up beside them, instantly gaining Deluxe's attention. He eyed the funny colored car and the two dudes inside, as they stared at the crew. He hated the fact that he'd left the now dirty .45 in Gator's car.

"Who the fuck them niggas?" Deluxe asked, as the two dudes finally passed by.

"I don't know. I ain't never seen 'em before," Myth added.

"They probably a few members of my fan club, 'cause you know muthafuckas be hatin'," Gator replied, walking back toward the guys with a bottle of Hennessey and a plastic shot glass. "At least we ain't got to worry about that faggot-ass Hughes no more," he continued, not giving anymore attention to the Cadillac or the passengers.

When Deluxe turned back around, the STS was completely out of sight.

"Shit now that I'm thinkin' 'bout it, I heard Hughes had a contract on his head since some shit went down between him and Premo's weak-ass crew last year. It was only a matter of time before somebody put his ass to sleep, so this couldn't have happened at a better time," Myth responded.

Realizing that no matter how hard he tried to forget that he'd just killed a cop, there was only one thing Deluxe could do to take his mind off of it, and that was to get some incredible hulk in him. He grabbed the Hennessey from his uncle and took it straight to the head, no cup, no ice, and no chaser. It was amazing what alcohol could do to help a person's mind feel at ease.

"Damn Nephew, I don't want yo' fuckin' backwash in my shit!" Gator yelled.

Ignoring his uncle's comment, Deluxe continued to turn the bottle upside down against his lips.

"Did this nigga hear me? Am I talkin' to myself?" Gator slightly mumbled to himself.

As Gator and Kane watched closely waiting for Deluxe to

stop, Myth saw a girl he knew and called her over. "Kandi…yo Kandi, what up? Come over here so I can holla at yo' fine ass for a second!" he yelled in his 250lb baritone voice. All the guys turned their head in her direction.

"Hey, I know that chick," Deluxe said, finally coming up for air. He handed the bottle back to his uncle and smiled. Gator didn't return the gesture.

Seeing Myth, Kandi's eyes lit up and she didn't hesitate following his orders. "What's up, Daddy?" she asked walking up.

She sported a form fitting pair of Seven Jeans and low cut Baby Phat shirt that showed her voluptuous D cup breast. Kandi's ass was so fat, she even made Melyssa Ford look like she had that white girl disease, no-ass-at-all. After giving Myth a hug, she turned around and looked at Deluxe. "Damn boy, you really been working out in the military huh? I ain't seen yo' ass in a while. When you get back in the D?" she asked eying his muscular physique.

"I been here a minute," Deluxe said nonchalantly. Kandi had a knack for running her big mouth too much. The last thing Deluxe wanted was for her to know exactly when he'd gotten in town so she could start gossiping, especially after what had just happened. "So, when did you change yo' shit to Kandi, Ms. Kiyanna?" he asked, revealing her real name.

She smiled. "Since I been a stripper at the club Déjà vu over on 8 Mile. Shit, yo' man Myth here is one of my favorite customers."

"Don't forget about me, Ma," Kane interjected.

Kandi sucked her teeth. "I mean you a'ight, but yo' ass still don't tip as much as big Myth." She walked over to Myth's 6'4' frame and hugged him again.

"Well that shit won't be for long," Kane added with a smirk.

Gator took a sip of Hennessey and finally spoke up. "How the fuck you supposed to do that? Let's not forget you just a foot solider in this operation, young boy. I ain't promoted yo' ass yet."

The two men stared at each other like raging bulls.

"Don't worry Gator, the work he gonna put in will have you rankin' his ass in no time," Myth stated in his cousin's defense.

"Yeah, we'll see," Gator said, taking another shot.

When Kandi seemed a bit uncomfortable, Deluxe decided to change the subject. "So, what made you become a stripper? I thought you went to Wayne University or some shit," he said, still surprised that one of his high school classmates had turned to the crazy profession.

"Cuz, I gotta get this paper," she replied, rubbing her hands together. "I did go to Wayne, but I ain't 'bout to work at no nine to five making that lil' bit of bread. Ain't that right, G-Money," Kandi said, turning toward Gator.

"You absolutely fuckin' right pretty lady." Gator raised the Hennessy bottle.

"Plus the bitches over there got some of the biggest asses I've seen," she added.

Deluxe's eyes were huge. "So, you gay too?"

"Shit, there's a lot of stuff you don't know about me. You shoulda gave me a chance back in the day." Kandi licked her lips and again eyed Deluxe's toned body and smooth chestnut brown skin. "Umm, I'm jealous. I know Rachelle gon' be glad to see your sexy ass." Kandi's smirk peeked through her full glossy lips. "Y'all still fucking right?"

"Look, I don't put my business out there like that," Deluxe shot back.

"Nigga I don't know what you being all secretive for, everybody know that shit," Kandi barked. "But the thing is, you need keep your eyes open cuz that bitch ain't as sweet as she seem."

Even though Deluxe was quite curious about what Kandi meant by her last statement, he decided not to comment. However, he still couldn't help but let his mind wander when thoughts floated around his head. Rachelle was his first real girlfriend and also his first piece of ass. They'd been together all throughout high school until Rachelle's mother sent her down south to live with her grandparents. Once that happened, it didn't take much to figure out Rachelle had been forced away because of him, especially since he was the descendant of one of Detroit's most famous drug dealer. However, when Rachelle turned twenty-one, she moved back to city, and the spark between the two love birds instantly ignited again. Now, even though they were no longer in a committed relationship, they still had sex every time Deluxe came home.

"You workin' tonight?" Myth asked Kandi, interrupting Deluxe's thoughts.

"Hell yeah. I work damn near every night. Shit, I ain't passing up no paper."

"Cool, I should be up there a lil' later once I handle some business, so keep that ass warm," Myth joked.

Kandi smiled. "Anything for you." She looked at Deluxe again. "Make sure you come see me too before you leave."

"I'll see what I can do," Deluxe replied, in his usual nonchalant tone.

All the men watched Kandi's enormous ass as she walked away.

"Now that's one fine bitch right there," Gator said, taking another shot of Hennessey.

"Yeah Ma got ass for days," Kane added, in his thick New York accent.

"I ain't never seen her in Déjà vu before," Gator stated.

Myth displayed a huge smile. "That's because yo' girl been clockin' you lately. Kandi been workin' for a minute, so I know yo' ass ain't took two steps in the buildin' if you missed her. Shit, she the baddest bitch up in there."

Gator shook his head. "You right. Mylani been ridin' a niggas dick extra hard." He laughed. I don't know why she be stressin' herself out like that though, 'cause I'ma do what the fuck I want. She may be my main girl, but I ain't never gon' be faithful to any bitch. She can forget that weak nigga theory."

He gave Myth and a pound and started laughing again. When Kane tried to join in, Gator shot him a cold look. "She on you real hard Nephew. How you know that bitch?"

"I knew her when she was a good girl. Back in high school," Deluxe replied. "She's been tryin' to fuck me forever."

"And you ain't hit that yet? Shit, she still a good girl," Myth countered.

"Hell yeah, and you know what. I'ma see how good she really is when I go up to Déjà vu, throw her money hungry-ass a few bunks, and fuck the shit outta her," Gator stated confidently.

"Not if I get to her first," Myth joked.

"Well if you do, wait for me, and we can have a fuckin' threesome," Gator boasted.

All four men burst into laughter. The surge of emotion felt particularly good to Deluxe, who'd finally gotten his mind off of Detective Hughes, and started to relax a bit. Feeling the effects from the constant shots, Gator gathered the crew to let them know it was time to make some moves and ride down to Plan B nightclub downtown. It was the place to be on a Sunday night and by this time the club should've been packed with the crews' prime choice of freaks ready to fuck for some money. It was also time to meet up with Gator's connect and handle some important business.

"Myth, I need you and Kane to switch cars wit' me, so y'all can drop off the bricks and the paper you just gave me. Make sure you split the bricks up between the two spots, then bring me fifty to hit Jimmy the Greek off. Once you done, meet me at the club," Gator instructed.

Myth looked at Gator like he was insane. "Fifty thousand? You jokin'? That ain't enough to pay him what we owe."

"Nigga I know that. You just do what I said, and I'll handle everythin' else. Oh, and get rid of that piece for me. It's wrapped up in a black towel, under the seat."

"Bet," Myth responded. "If you need mine, you know where to find it."

He and Kane turned around at the same time and walked away. A few seconds later, they jumped inside Gator's car and drove off.

As soon as Deluxe sat in the passenger's seat of Myth's car, he didn't waste anytime drilling his uncle about Kane. It was an unwritten rule that Detroit natives had a deep hatred for outsiders, especially anyone from New York. "So, what's up wit' the New York nigga, Unc? I thought you didn't want anybody from outside the D workin' wit' the fam?"

"Yeah I know. Let's just say I did this shit for Myth. He begged me to let that muthafucka up in the organization. He claims that Kane gone be pullin' his weight and then some, but I ain't seen the shit yet. He more of a bitch if anythin'."

"Well, I can tell you now that it's somethin' about his grimey-ass that rubs me the wrong way. I don't trust that cat."

Gator hit the steering wheel with one of his hands. "I don't trust his bitch-ass either, so that's why I need you to keep an eye on him for me."

"How am I supposed to do that from North Carolina?" Deluxe questioned.

"Easy. Don't go the fuck back. I could really use someone wit' your skills as my top enforcer."

Deluxe looked at Gator strangely. "And get a dishonorable discharge from the Marines. Shit, I don't know about that, Unc."

"Nigga, I was the one who told you to go in the fuckin' service to begin wit'! You think I told you to do that just so you could serve your country and shit?"

"No, but..."

"But what," Gator continued. "You were trained so the fam could have a marksman on board...a muthafuckin' professional. After puttin' in work tonight, I see you more than ready, so fuck the Marines. You can make way more money workin' for me anyway."

Damn, and here I was thinking he wanted me to go into the military to get off the streets. Guess I was wrong, Deluxe thought as they continued on their way downtown. He felt proud that Gator thought enough of his skills to offer him a lead position in the organization. Although he was hesitant, a part of him felt obligated to accept the job. Gator wasn't one who took no for an answer, so Deluxe was definitely stuck between a gun and a hard place.

CHAPTER 3

By the time Gator and Deluxe pulled up in front of Plan B, the line was already wrapped around the building. Gator laughed as he watched all the fake high rollers trying to act like they could afford the $50.00 VIP parking fee, while the weekend hustlers, who'd only made enough money to buy a club outfit and a pair of Nike Air Force Ones blasted their wannabe anthem, '*Ballin*' by Jim Jones.

Deluxe turned to his uncle. "You think I need to grab Myth's piece?"

"No need. Jimmy's security ain't gon' allow you to take that shit up in his spot. We should be good." Gator rolled down the window and yelled for the head of security. A few seconds later, a burly 6'9' Shaq looking dude approached Gator's side of the car.

"What's up Gator?" the guard greeted.

"Tell both of them punk-ass parking attendants to make sure they don't park my shit next to no one else's," Gator instructed, as he slid the security guard a crispy $100 bill. "Keep the change."

"You know I got you G. Jimmy the Greek is waiting for you in his office," the massive baby Shaq look-a-like said, while opening up the car door to usher Gator out.

"Come on Nephew. Let's see which one of these hoes you gon' fuck tonight." Gator slapped Deluxe on his back when he got out the car.

As the pair walked to the front door they could see the looks on the lame-ass cornball faces, wishing they had the clout or the money Gator and his crew were known for flashing. The ten carat platinum bracelet with VVS canary yellow stones and the diamond encrusted Jesus piece Gator wore was even more of a reason to attract haters.

It looked like a scene straight out of New Jack City with Nino and G-Money, as Gator and Deluxe made their way into the newly renovated club and through the crowded dance floor of half-naked women shaking their asses to Luke's old school song, 'Doo Doo Brown'. The DJ, G. Chandler from the radio station turned down the music slightly to send a shout out to Gator as he and Deluxe shifted through the crowd on their way upstairs. Once they were searched for weapons, the two security guards outside Jimmy the Greek's office, let them inside.

"Hey, look who finally showed up. Sonny, go get me a couple of bottles of Dom Pérignon, and bring up a few of my Cuban cigars. Oh, and tell that broad Tipsy to send six of her best girls up here right now," a raspy voice ordered with authority, when Gator and Deluxe walked through the door. "Gator, good to see you, sit down," Jimmy the Greek said, with excitement as they made their way over to the plush white leather sofas that were eloquently arranged in the room. "Who's this with you?" Jimmy asked, with a bit of concern in his voice. "Where's Myth and that new fella you got working for you. The one from New York?"

"Myth and Kane should be here in a minute, but this is my nephew Deluxe, the soldier me and Myth was tellin' you about from the Marines. He gonna be a real good addition to the fam," Gator said, to the gray haired slimy looking Greek man who hadn't taken his eyes off of Deluxe.

Jimmy had the look of the average Greek guy from the little section of downtown Detroit known as Greek Town. He was short, overweight, with a round beer belly and a pointy nose. Straight from the gate there was something that Deluxe definitely didn't like about him.

"Marines huh? I hear that they are the best. Come over here, and let me shake your hand young fella. My father always told me you can tell a lot about a man by shaking his hand," Jimmy said to Deluxe in a commanding voice.

With all the force that he could muster, Deluxe shook the

Greek's hand with the intent of squeezing his cold, slimy, fat fingers until he cut off the circulation.

"Nice grip you got there," Jimmy squealed, pulling from Deluxe's grip. "Come let's celebrate," Jimmy yelled while rubbing his hand

Just then, Myth walked through the door holding onto the Alan's Shoe store bag.

"Hey, another part of the crew is here," Jimmy announced.

"Where the hell is Kane?" Gator asked. He watched as Myth placed the bag on the table in front of Jimmy.

Myth shook his head. "Tryin' to get wit' one of those freaks out there."

"So you gonna let this nigga disrespect the fam like that? We got business to handle and he out there tryin' to get some ass!" Gator yelled. "You know what Myth, you better check yo' fuckin' cousin before I do. I already don't like that corny muthafucka."

"Yeah I got you. I'll be sure to talk to his ass," Myth responded. *Damn, I hope it wasn't a mistake bringin' this nigga on board.* Myth knew sometimes Kane could be a hand full, and no matter what he told him to do, sometimes he just wouldn't listen.

Sonny walked back in the room with the bottles that Jimmy ordered, along with six of the baddest bitches the city of Detroit had to offer. The one with an enormous ass instantly got Deluxe's dick's attention. She wore a pink bra with a matching pair of thongs that seemed to show her well groomed pussy through the fabric. The look on her face showed that she noticed the way Deluxe stared at her, so she didn't waste any time walking over to him and immediately took position on his lap.

"They call me Suga, but you can call me all yours. What's your name, Daddy?" she whispered in his ear.

"Deluxe," he replied, trying to remain as cool as a fan while Suga massaged his throbbing dick with her ass. He moved her long platinum blond wig out of his face.

"Umm Deluxe huh, is that because of this?" Suga asked, as she continued to move her hips back and forth. Before Deluxe could manage to respond, Suga jumped up, turned around and went directly for his belt buckle.

"Hold up, you gonna do this shit right here?" Deluxe questioned, looking around. His eyes scanned the room, and just as he thought, everyone seemed to be looking at him with huge smiles on their faces, especially Gator. He looked like a proud parent.

"Don't be scared Nephew. We ain't gon' laugh at that lil' dick you got!" Gator yelled.
Myth, Jimmy the Greek, and a few of the women all started laughing.

By that time Suga had unzipped Deluxe's pants and pulled

his shaft out of his Calvin Klein boxers. Her eyes almost extended to the size of golf balls. "Shit, this man is hung like a fucking horse, so all y'all lil' dick niggas, need to stop laughing before you get embarrassed. He got one of them porn star dicks."

The moment Deluxe heard Suga bragging on his manhood, he suddenly began to feel more comfortable. If it was one thing he was proud of as a man, it was his huge dick. Over the years, he'd always gotten compliments on what he considered nothing short of perfection. His shaft had just the right length, width and texture. Even the small mole that rested just below the head had a sexy Cindy Crawford thing going that all the women seemed to love.

"Yeah, I'ma enjoy this," Suga said, as she quickly began to deep-throat all ten inches of Deluxe's dick as if her life depended on it.

Gator began laughing and nudged Myth with his elbow. "If that bitch is excited about Deluxe, she need to come slob on my massive tool," he bragged, rubbing his crotch area.

Even though there were five other women in the room, they struggled to get all the men's attention away from Suga, whose large drops of salvia dripped out of her mouth as she sucked and jerked Deluxe's dick intensively.

Enjoying the feeling of complete pleasure, Deluxe closed his eyes and tilted his head back while Suga continued to work her

magic. The loud slurping sounds she made started to arouse everyone in the room, including a club waitress who'd only stopped by
to drop off extra champagne glasses. As Suga picked up the pace
and continued to bob her head up and down his dick, Deluxe could
feel his climax approaching. Within a matter of seconds, his warm
thick cum exploded into Suga's mouth, causing Deluxe to jerk uncontrollably. She swallowed every ounce not wanting to waste any
on Jimmy's expensive couch.

"Now that's what the fuck I'm talkin' about. I'm next!"
Gator yelled, just as Suga came up for air. He was preparing to
unzip his pants when Jimmy stopped him.

"Listen, I don't have time to sit here and watch you guys
get your dicks sucked all night. Let's take care of business first,
and then we can have some fun." He looked over at Suga who was
wiping her mouth. "Good job, honey. I'll make sure that young
gentleman gives you a nice tip."

Deluxe looked over at Jimmy. *I don't need you to fuckin'
tell her what I'm gonna do, fat ass.* He could see Gator looking at
him out the corner of his eye. His cold stare told Deluxe to be cool,
which he did instantly. However, if it was anything he needed to
know, Deluxe was sure that his uncle would put him up on the
game later.

"Oh, she's gonna be taken care of for servicin' my family

like that," Gator responded. He walked over to Suga and peeled off two one hundred dollar bills. "There's more where that came from. When I'm finished wit' my business sweetheart, I want the same thing off the menu."

Gator smiled causing the craters on his cheeks to become even more visible. His alligator looking skin was another reason why he'd been penned with his famous nickname.

"Damn, what a way to end the night fellas," Deluxe said, zipping up his pants.

"What a way to end the night, you hear this kid Sonny," Jimmy the Greek replied, while pouring the glasses full of champagne.

The short Greek man was really starting to test Deluxe's patience.

After passing the champagne glasses around the room, Jimmy took the Mr. Alan's bag that had been placed in front of him, and dumped the contents all over the expensive marble and Italian table.

Myth swallowed his champagne in one huge gulp. He knew Jimmy wasn't going to be pleased, and hoped the Greek man didn't think it was his idea. He hated when Gator took unnecessary risks.

Jimmy threw several stacks of money in the air. "If this is

some type of joke, I'm not laughing. Where's the rest of my fucking money?"

"Let's talk in the other part of yo' office for a minute Jimmy," Gator commented.

"Yeah, that's a great idea," Jimmy the Greek replied. "Ladies you need to leave." His tone changed instantly. He rushed into another room located in his office with Sonny right on his trail.

"Deluxe, relax for a minute. We'll be right back!" Gator shouted as he and Myth hurried behind Jimmy, and then closed the door.

Before going back out to the club to make her rounds, Suga wrote something down on a piece of paper then walked over to Deluxe and whispered in his ear. "I ain't supposed to do this, but here's my phone number, call me if you wanna finish what we started," she said, in a soft seductive voice. She handed the piece of paper to Deluxe before blowing him a kiss.

"I'll try," Deluxe remarked, not really fazed by the attention. He'd seen her kind before and really wasn't interested.

No sooner than Suga walked out of the office, Deluxe heard what appeared to be yelling coming from the second room in Jimmy the Greek's office. A few seconds later, Gator stormed out with the rest of the men right behind him.

"First of all, you come up in my spot without all my fucking money for those keys you just got. Now you wanna walk out on me without being dismissed?" Jimmy shouted, with offensive hand gestures. "Gator, listen you're making too much noise around the city, especially with you buying all those fucking expensive ass cars. How many do you own now, five…six? You need to calm down a little bit," Jimmy edged. "You see that's the problem with niggas Sonny, you give them an inch and they try to steal a mile! I can't let you continue to move this much coke every week if you gonna continue to act like a fucking nigga!"

"Let me? What the fuck do you mean let me? Lets get one thing fuckin' straight, you don't let me do shit muthafucka! These streets are mine. I can easily find me another connect, so don't get it twisted fat man. If it wasn't for me, yo' slimy-ass wouldn't be makin' the fuckin' money you makin'. Keep talkin' to me like that and I'll show you how much of a nigga I can be."

Despite Gator's blatant disrespect, Jimmy still smiled. "Maybe you should be more like your brother, Rock. He was way more respectful than you. He also had more class."

Gator clenched his jaw. "Don't you ever fuckin' compare me to my brother you gyro eatin' muthafucka!"

Jimmy the Greek had been Rock and Gator's connect for years and everyone knew after Rock died, it was only a matter of time before the two men bumped heads. Not only were they both hot heads, but as Gator's grip on the streets of Detroit grew stronger, his desire to flaunt his new wealth grew as well. Spending $20,000 at the local casino poker tables, expensive cars, and extravagant shopping trips was normal for Gator, but this new behavior made Jimmy the Greek very uneasy. He'd seen far too many times where flashiness caused unnecessary indictments to get handed down from a federal grand jury.

"You remember this one thing, never ever bite the hand that feeds you, nigga. You remember that," Jimmy said, in a stern voice. "Now you better bring me the rest of my fucking money or else!"

"Let's roll!" Gator yelled to Myth and Deluxe.

However, before they could even get out of the door, Jimmy said something to Sonny in their native Greek language, then turned to face the men. "Myth, you seem to have your head on a little straighter than your friend does. A wise man once told me that when it rains, it pours, and it pours on those that don't have umbrellas. When it's all said and done your fucking mooley friend, Gator will get what he deserves," Jimmy said to Myth, who was almost outside the door.

Myth turned around and looked back at Jimmy. "Jimmy you cool, but no matter what, I'ma always roll wit' my fam."

CHAPTER 4

The long ride back to Gator's house over on the east side of the city, gave Deluxe plenty of time to think. With all of the money that Gator was getting, Deluxe never understood why he hadn't moved out to one of Detroit's fancy suburbs like Royal Oak or Bloomfield Township. Whenever Deluxe would ask him, Gator would always say, "I'm the heart of the city, why would I ever leave? Plus any nigga runnin' up on me gotta get past my gate first, and if they do, God help 'em cause I got some serious heat for they ass."

As much as his uncle supplied South East Michigan with good coke, Deluxe figured he would want to have his resting place as far away from the dirt and grime of the streets as much as possible. One thing that Deluxe knew about Gator was that he was real loyal, that's why he didn't understand what had just gone down with Jimmy the Greek. Under normal circumstances, Deluxe didn't usually ask Gator a lot of questions regarding his operation, but this time he had to know.

"What happened back at the club, Unc?" Deluxe asked, with obvious concern in his voice.

"That fuckin' Greek pussy thinks that I'm one of his flunkies or some shit, that's what happened. He's pissed off cause I ain't pay him all the money that I owe, but I did that shit on purpose. Hell, since he talked to me like that, now I'm really gonna pay his ass when I get ready. That muthafucka ain't gon' tell me how many cars I need to have. Fuck him!"

Deluxe was shocked. He had no idea Gator was that shady when it came down to business. However, he also thought maybe that was the reason why his uncle was so successful in the game.

"So, what if he tries to come at you?"

Gator frowned. "Me? Nigga, I'm protected. If he comes at me, he's comin' at all of us! Hopefully that's where you come in anyway."

Deluxe didn't respond.

"Man fuck him and his dick ridin' partner, Sonny. Little does Jimmy know, his ass is just as expendable as the next muthafucka. I been needin' to get a cheaper supplier anyway. Actually, the more I process this shit, I think it's about that time for me to take a trip to go see my man, Chico."

"Who the fuck is Chico?"

Gator had no words for Deluxe, just laughter.

With that he whipped out his cell phone and dialed a series of numbers. "Chico, hola," Gator said, to the person on the other end of the phone. "I need a face to face ASAP, what's the weather like in Mexico?" he asked, while letting out another hearty laugh.

Gator had met Chico a year earlier while vacationing in Acapulco with his girl and apparently they'd hit it off real good and had talked about more than just the beautiful Mexican women that Acapulco had to offer.

"Oh, you moved to Cabo San Lucas huh? I heard it's beautiful there." Gator paused. "That sounds good. I'll get my girl to book me a flight, and I'll call you later wit' a update." After another cheerful laugh, Gator hung up.

By eavesdropping on the conversation, Deluxe knew some shit was going to pop off with Gator getting a new connect, so he had to be ready for whatever could possibly go down.

Moments later, the duo pulled up to a stainless steel digital keypad at the end of Gator's driveway. Gator reached his hand out of the window and punched in a five digit code. They waited patiently as the black iron gate slowly opened.

Gator pulled onto a circular driveway which led to his five bedroom 7000 sq ft. house that sat nestled in a premiere location of Grosse Pointe Shores. The yard had perfectly manicured grass, uniformed trimmed bushes, and a flower bed of fresh red roses, that could've very well been in a Better Homes and Gardens magazine. With one push of a button the doors to a massive four car garage opened up revealing what looked like an exhibit at an international car show. Deluxe smiled as Gator slowly pulled into the exceptionally clean garage and placed the car in park. There was a silver Maserati Gran Sport sitting on chrome 23" Giovanni rims and an all black Ashton Martin DB9 parked next to it. As many times as he'd been to his uncle's house, Deluxe's dick still got hard every time he laid eyes on the top of the line luxury cars. Even the deep metallic red BMW 650i Coupe that Gator had purchased for his girl Mylani was nice.

Both Gator and Deluxe got out of the car as the garage door slowly closed. When they headed past the custom painted Suzki Hayabusa GSXR 1300 motorcycle and toward the entrance of the house, Gator stopped.

"Meet me down in the basement. I gotta talk to you 'bout somethin' before you shut down for the night. I'ma run up and fuck wit' Mylani for a minute, then I'll be down there," he informed. "Oh yeah nigga what you did tonight was priceless, so here you go, this should be enough for your services," he said, while tossing his nephew a stack of freshly wrapped hundred dollar bills.

"Thanks Unc, but you didn't have to do this. I owe you my

life," Deluxe replied, flipping through the crisp bills. *Damn this is at least ten thousand.*

He normally got money from Gator for doing jobs here and there, but this was his biggest payment yet.

"Shit, I know that, but I take care of my fam, nigga. Remember that."

Deluxe walked behind Gator as he entered the house and turned off the alarm. "Don't' forget to take yo' shoes off. I'm tryin' to get some pussy from Mylani tonight, so I don't need to hear her damn mouth if she see any dirt on the carpet. Her eyes are like a fuckin' microscope when it comes to that shit."

Gator definitely had money, cars, and some of the baddest women, which made him the envy of most men in Detroit, but his house was over the top. Mylani had done her best to make the house look like more than an average hustler's bachelor pad. As one of the cities number one real estate agents, Mylani not only made a lot of money herself, but she also had the exquisite taste that went along with that title.

Deluxe quickly followed the no shoes rule, then walked straight to the gourmet kitchen as Gator ran upstairs. The kitchen floor was tiled in a beautiful aurora marble, which could be heated during the cold winter months along with matching marble counter tops and hanging pendant lights, which always contributed to a peaceful ambiance in the room.

Deluxe walked by the six burner Viking stove and stopped at the stainless steel sub zero refrigerator that his uncle kept stocked with bottles of Armand de Brignac Champagne, or 'Ace of Spades' as it was affectionately known. He grabbed a cold Heineken to help him unwind while he waited for Gator. After taking off the beer cap with his hands, Deluxe walked out of the kitchen and down the staircase which led to the basement; a place in which he called a man's paradise, and his favorite part of the house. To add to his flashiness, Gator had the space decked out with a custom-made, nine foot pool table with his name engraved in the center, a state of the art movie room which displayed a ceiling recessed projection screen, leather reclining seats, surround sound and of course a full sized Italian marbled top bar that was always fully stocked with Remy Martin Louis XIII Cognac. To set off the whole gangsta vibe, the walls were lined with several pictures of Al Pacino in his famous Scarface and Carlito's Way movies in big expensive wood frames.

However, what Deluxe loved most of all about the space were the many pictures of Gator and his father that were placed around the room. Rock and Gator were only two years apart in age, but you would've thought they were siamese twins by how often they were together.

As he continued to stare at the picture of the only two men he'd ever loved with all his heart, Gator walked in. "Yeah I miss my nigga Rock. Lord help them fools who set him up, but trust me, when I find out who did that shit, I'm killin' 'em, and everyone they love. That's my word!"

"Yeah, I still can't believe you never found out who killed pops after all these years."

Gator shook his head. "I know, but don't worry, eventually the streets will talk, and we'll get them niggas. In due time, Nephew. In due time."

Talking about his deceased father always made him angry, so Deluxe decided to change the subject. "So what's the word? What you need to get at me about? I'm tired as hell and would love to forget about tonight."

"Well that's what I need to rap to you about. See the fam has been makin' big moves into territories that were once off limits, but now have become necessary real estate. Ya feel me?" Gator asked with a serious expression.

"Unc, I know where this is going."

"Good, cause the bigger we get, the bigger the problems. The bigger the problems, there's a bigger need for solution. Now your pops never wanted you in the business, but we need you. You showed me tonight that you got the heart of a fuckin' lion and the skill of a sniper." Before Deluxe could open his mouth Gator quickly said, "I don't trust anyone else to handle things for the fam at this point, but you. Plus it's only a matter of time before I get at Jimmy the Greek, or he tries to get at me."

Deluxe sat on the edge of the plush leather sofa contemplating what he was about to say. He'd gone to the military hoping to get away from the murderous lifestyle that he was surrounded by in the streets, but it looked as if he wasn't gonna be able to dodge it. He'd even learned his first lesson in killing when Gator took him to the morgue to see what had happened to his father. It was there when Gator told him that it is always better to do the shooting than to be shot at.

Over the years, Deluxe often wondered why Gator had taken him to see his father's lifeless body on the cold metal table, but now it was finally becoming clear. Deluxe thought during the years that his uncle had spent time teaching him about the streets was to groom him, so he could handle his own. However, now he could clearly see that he was wrong. The reason was to turn Deluxe into a heartless, cold-blooded, executioner for the fam. However, even though Gator had taught him how to shoot his first gun, it was the Marine Corps that taught him how to kill in cold blood. A Marine Corps Sniper was considered the cream of the crop, and Deluxe was known for being the best that a sniper had to offer. With this in mind, Deluxe decided it was only right that he be the enforcer Gator needed.

At that point, despite Deluxe's reservations, he knew what had to be done. "What are the terms?" Deluxe asked, confirming his willingness to become the organizations' hit man.

"That's what the fuck I'm talkin' about Nephew. You name it, you got it," Gator replied, with the excitement of a man who'd just plunged into his first piece of pussy.

Contemplating the terms in his head, Deluxe looked Gator in his eyes and in a stern matter of fact voice, and laid out his own terms. "No children, under no circumstances. I ain't killin' no fuckin' kids."

"That's workable. Anythin' else?"

"Yeah. I need you to help me find out who killed my pops. I gotta make they ass pay," the newly hired gunman answered, as Gator looked at him, puzzled by his nephews last requirement.

Hmmm… I can never let Deluxe find out what I know about Rock's death, Gator thought to himself before replying, "No doubt. We'll get them muthafucka's soon enough. Get some rest, it's been a long night," Gator suggested, giving Deluxe a pound to seal the deal.

After leaving Deluxe in the basement, Gator walked up-stairs thinking about Deluxe's request to know who killed his father. For years he'd avoided having the conversation with his nephew. Gator knew that if Deluxe ever knew the truth behind his father's murder, there would be repercussions that could prove to be detrimental to the family. Being the closest thing to a father that Deluxe had known, Gator refused to lose his nephew's trust by telling him anything regarding the murder. Besides, he had business that needed to be taken care of, and Gator damn sure wasn't going to let anything stand in the way of accomplishing his mission.

Snapping out of the daze, Gator approached his office in another wing of the house and quickly thought about the business that he needed Deluxe to take care of. A heartless kingpin, Gator wanted to keep his hands clean from all of the killings as much as possible. He figured it would be harder for a prosecutor to get a conviction if he was never the one caught pulling the trigger. Bringing Deluxe into the family to be a hired gunman couldn't have come at a better time for Gator and his operation, especially since there was an organization, MGB or Money Getting Boyz, who were trying to make a come up on the east side of the city.

Normally Gator wouldn't have paid much attention to dudes trying to get money, but the MGB crew was starting to make some serious noise and showed little respect for the reigning king of the city. Word on the street was, the leader of MGB, was a young nigga named Premo, who was getting his supply from another dealer out of Flint, cutting Gator out of the deal, which was a huge no-no. Gator was determined to send a deadly message to any organization in the city that tried to deal in Detroit without going through him or Myth. He didn't really care that the young dudes were trying to lace their pockets with money, the problem was he wasn't getting a cut, and that type of disrespect wouldn't fly without severe consequences. Sending Deluxe to see Premo was high on Gator's priority list. He knew that if he had Premo, or one of his lieutenants killed, the rest of the city would think twice about getting their work from someone other than himself.

Gator reached into his pocket to retrieve a set of keys, which opened one of his most prized possessions, his desk. A place where most of his cherished porno tapes were hidden from Mylani. After placing the small key into the two thousand dollar executive desk drawer, he pulled out an ounce of coke and smiled. Another one of his esteemed possessions that he hid from his girl, and everyone else who knew him.

"I couldn't wait to get home to be wit' you," he grinned.

Gator sat down in his leather reclining chair, then opened the plastic bag before placing a large amount of coke on the dark cherry wood piece of furniture. He chopped the white powder up a little, then slid it in a neat straight line. Gator grabbed a straw that had been cut in half from the pen holder, then proceeded to snort the coke up his nostrils. The high powered drug felt good as it quickly traveled through his body and into his bloodstream; a feeling Gator had been experiencing since his brother died. So far, he'd managed to keep his daily routine away from everyone, but surely he knew the nasty habit was bound to surface at some point.

CHAPTER 5

"Jayson, I know you hear me. Jayson!" Deluxe heard a voice yelling from the top of the stairs. It was annoying when anybody called him by his real name.

"Yeah," Deluxe replied, still groggy from not having enough sleep. After looking at several of Gator's large collection of movies all night, it felt as if he'd only been sleep for five minutes.

"I'm fixing breakfast, so get yourself together. Momma Ruth is on her way over here," Mylani yelled.

"A'ight gimmie ten more minutes," he pleaded.

"Boy don't make me send Gerald down there to get you. Get up," she said with a slight laugh.

Deluxe finally opened his eyes and laughed to himself a little bit at the thought of Mylani being the only person in the world able to call Gator by his government name. Anybody else would've been dealt with. When he looked around the room, it didn't take long to realize that he'd fallen asleep in the movie theatre.

"Damn, these are some comfortable chairs," Deluxe said to

himself. He stared at the plush black recliner and rubbed his hand against the buttery leather material. "If I didn't know any better, I would'a thought I was at the Ritz Carlton or some shit."

Getting up out of the chair, Deluxe stretched his arms before walking up the stairs. When he reached the foyer which contained stunning vaulted ceilings, he continued up another flight of stairs to the third floor, where the guest bedroom was located. Deluxe didn't waste anytime walking into the spacious guest bathroom and immediately began brushing his teeth. Moments later, he took off his clothes then stepped inside the huge walk-in shower with luxury limestone tile, a 10" Moen shower head and four body sprayers. It was like being in a spa.

While Deluxe let the warm water massage his muscles, he contemplated everything that had transpired from the night before. From the keys in the trunk, the dead cop that was now probably plastered over every news channel, the drama between Jimmy the Greek, and the position that Gator had offered him, Deluxe realized that a lot of shit had gone down in just one night. As the water began to travel down to his dick, he imagined what it would feel like to have Rachelle wash his chiseled body. He'd been in town for a couple of days and had yet to call her because he knew she would want to monopolize his time by fucking all day, and that wouldn't have sat too well with Gator, especially since there was so much business to take care of.

After fantasizing about Rachelle and thoroughly washing his body, Deluxe turned off the water, then stepped out the shower. By this time, he could hear a high pitched laugh coming from downstairs and knew exactly who it was. He looked in the mirror and brushed the waves that had formed on his head from wearing his doo-rag most nights, before hurrying around the room to get dressed. Minutes later, Deluxe walked down the steps wearing his favorite white Polo shirt, dark blue jean shorts and a huge smile because he was extremely excited about seeing the guest of honor. Once he entered the dining room, he walked directly over to his grandmother and gave her a huge hug. The embrace seemed to last forever.

"Baby you need to take better care of yourself. Look at those bags under your eyes," she said, once Deluxe gave her back some circulation. It had been a while since Momma Ruth had seen her only grandson.

"That's why I love you Granny. You always look out for me," Deluxe spoke as he gave her a kiss on the cheek. He seemed to tower over her petite frail frame.

"I'm so glad that you had a chance to come and visit for a while. Look at you, your father would be so proud. God rest his soul. Now don't be getting into no trouble out here with your no good uncle. I know you done idolized him all your life, but now you got a good thang going for yourself in that Marines stuff, so don't screw up. You hear me boy!" Momma Ruth said with a stern voice.

"Come on Momma can we not do this today?" Gator asked, as he walked into the room. He walked over and tried to give Momma Ruth a kiss, but she shooed him away.

Momma Ruth tossed her long gray hair over her shoulder. "Don't be talking to your mother like that boy. You know what Gerald Green, you can still go over my knee."

"Momma, please," Gator pleaded. He knew how outspoken his mother could be, which got on his nerves majority of the time.

"Don't momma please me boy, and don't go messing up Jayson's life with all your foolishness." She turned to Deluxe. "You know I really wish your father was here to see how much of a good man you turned out to be. Don't disappoint him, or me."

Deluxe immediately felt guilty, but tried not to let it show. "I won't Granny."

At that moment, Mylani walked into the room carrying a tray of pancakes. The rest of the food which consisted of bacon, eggs, biscuits and grits were already on the table. "Is everybody ready to eat?" she asked, placing the tray down.

"You know Gerald, I don't even think you realize how

good this woman is to you," Momma Ruth said. "Every time I come over here, Mylani's cooking a hot meal for your sorry butt. When are y'all gonna get married and have some kids, so I can have another grandbaby? What are you waiting on? For me to die?"

Gator immediately shook his head.

"I don't know what's taking him so long to marry me, Momma Ruth. We've been dating long enough. I think Gerald is happy just doing the Oprah and Stedman thing," Mylani replied. Her beautiful smile seemed to warm the room. The auburn hair which ran down her back matched her smooth copper skin tone and hazel colored eyes.

"Mylani don't add to this," Gator replied, feeling somewhat embarrassed. He hated when they ganged up on him. "Can we just eat already?"

"Yeah, sit down everybody, and let's eat before I have to knock this boy out," Momma Ruth insisted. After everyone took their seats, she proceeded to bless the table with a long prayer that included a request to keep her only grandson safe from harm and away from Gator.

• •

It hadn't even been a good ten minutes into breakfast when Gator started getting calls back to back from Myth on his cell phone. He ignored the first three calls, not wanting to hear his mother's mouth, but when the phone wouldn't stop ringing, he finally jumped up and walked into another room.

"That boy is so rude," Momma Ruth said, putting a piece of bacon into her mouth.

Several minutes later, Gator quickly walked back into the room. "Come on Deluxe, there's a problem at the office," he announced without warning.

Momma Ruth's wrinkled face frowned. "What? Well you better tell some of those people that work for you to take care of it. We trying to eat like a normal family."

"No Momma, there's a problem wit' payroll. If I don't get it straight ain't nobody gettin' paid today and you know how black people are about they money."

Momma Ruth gave him a look that said she knew he was lying. "Boy, you better not be getting your nephew into no mess. You know Ronald would be turning over in his grave if he knew his son was in the street. Don't disregard your brother's wishes."

"I'm not. Now we gotta go," Gator said. He walked over and gave both Mylani and Momma Ruth a kiss on the cheek. Deluxe did the same.

"Bye baby, be careful," Momma Ruth said to Deluxe, as he walked out the room. She didn't say a word to her son.

Deluxe watched as Gator grabbed a black towel from another one of his cars. At that point he knew the phone call must've been serious. However, he waited until they got into the car and pulled out the garage before he asked what was going on. "What's the deal Unc?"

Looking perplexed as they waited for the front gate to open, Gator finally spoke in a confused voice. "Myth called and said that one of my dope houses on the west side got hit about five this mornin'. So you ready to put in more work, 'cause I want whoever did this to be in a fuckin' coffin."

He didn't waste time opening the towel and placing the Glock 35 with an extended barrel on Deluxe's lap. Once the gate opened, Gator immediately sped down the street like a drag racer.

"Yeah, I'm ready," Deluxe answered grabbing the gun.

"Good, you hold on to that piece 'cause I got my own this time," Gator said, patting his waist. "We need extra enforcement on this one."

After riding in silence for the next ten minutes the two pulled up to East Side Drywall & Company, Gator's legit business that he used to wash all the drug money he raked in. When they pulled into the parking lot, Gator parked the CLS on the side of the building and searched the parking lot with his blood shot eyes for anything that looked out of the ordinary. However, the only thing he noticed was Myth's Lexus parked next to a dumpster. Gator jumped out of his car and slammed the door with such force the entire car shook. Deluxe knew things were about to pop off, so he quickly jumped out as well and followed Gator inside the building.

Walking past the empty receptionist desk, the two men headed straight for the conference room in the back of the office. With an overloading amount of anger, Gator stormed into the room. The air was so tense that it could've been cut with a knife as Gator walked around the room and stopped in front of Myth.

"How in the fuck did this shit happen? Can you or your damn cousin explain that shit to me?" He pounded his fist into the oak table, and then turned his head toward Kane. Nobody said a word. "Since neither one of y'all niggas ain't got shit to say somebody 'bout to lose they fuckin' life right now!" He gave Deluxe a look, which instantly prompted Myth to speak up.

"All we know right now is that the spot got hit, but we gon' find out who did it though and handle that shit," Myth exclaimed, taking the attention off Kane, who looked like he could care less.

"You fuckin' right yo' ass is gonna find out who did this shit, and when you do, I want they ass brought to me!" Gator walked to the head of the large table, took a seat, then looked back at Kane. "How the fuck did this shit happen? You supposed to be in charge of the west side dope house, muthafucka?"

"It happened when I stepped out," Kane responded noncha-lantly.

"What the fuck do you mean, it happened when you stepped out! Nigga, you supposed to be on point at all times. You know yo' ass can't leave the spot unless me, Myth or at least an-other foot solider is there to relieve you. How could you be so fuckin' stupid?" Before Kane could even part his lips, Gator con-tinued. "How much of my shit did they get?"

"All twelve bricks and all the money. About $200,000 large?" Kane replied, with a slight smirk on his face.

As dark as Gator was, his face still seemed to turn a mix-ture of red and purple.

Once Deluxe thought about the street value that had been stolen, he knew that Myth and Kane were about to feel the wrath of the cities most infamous boss. His uncle had gotten his nickname Gator, in part because of his skin and love for alligator shoes, but it was also because of his merciless dealings on the street, and rip-ping niggas to shreds. He would stalk his prey and without warning attack and torture them with more vile than anyone. That's why it just didn't make sense that someone would be dumb enough, or even brave enough, to steal from him. In any case someone had to pay dearly for it, not only with their life, but even more so with the lives of those they loved the most.

Standing up and flipping over the oak table with immense force, Gator pulled out his nickel-plated 9mm pistol from his waist and shoved it into the side of Kane's head.

"Is somethin' funny muthafucka?" Gator asked, while Kane threw his hands in the air. "I just got hit for damn near half of the twenty-five bricks I just got, and most of my fuckin' bread…And you gonna sit here wit' a smirk on yo' damn face?"

Myth jumped up. "Gator what the fuck man? Kane ain't mean nothin' behind that shit. Put the fuckin' gun away. You know how he likes to joke around."

Making a mental note of the fact that he just had a gun pointed at his head, Kane quickly agreed. "Yeah son, calm down B. It ain't even like that."

"Well you better stop tryin' to be fuckin' Steve Harvey up in this bitch, baby boy!" He removed the gun from Kane's head. "Nigga you better go get every ounce of my shit back, and every fuckin' penny of my money, then bring those cock suckers to me!"

Before Gator could finish laying down the law his cell phone started ringing. Looking at the caller ID he sighed. "What does this muthafucka want?" he said out loud, before opening the phone. "What?"

"The streets are already talking Gator, so is there anything I need to be concerned about? After all, you're missing a lot of money right now, and I hope none of it's mine," the voice on the other end of the phone demanded.

Gator wondered how word had gotten back to Jimmy the Greek about the robbery already. "Look, I'm in the middle of a meetin'. I can't talk about this shit right now!"

"You know, I only gave you a pass last night on the strength of your brother. You should be dead, and now my patience is wearing thin. I want the rest of my fucking money Gator. I'd hate to send my boys over to your house to rape your girl, then disfigure her fucking body."

The next thing Gator heard was a click.

Damn I could really use a hit right now, Gator thought as he closed his phone and shoved it into the pocket of his all black Sean Jean sweat pants.

"Myth, you and Kane get the fuck outta my face," he said, looking at each one of them. "Oh, and Myth, either you or your bitch-ass cousin better find out who's responsible for this shit, and bring them to me, today!" Gator scolded.

Even though Myth was still pissed about Gator placing a gun to Kane's head, he managed to calm down a bit. "Trust me, we'll find 'em." Myth then nodded his head as he exited the room with Kane close behind.

"Deluxe, I don't trust that nigga Kane. I want you to find

out if his gold teeth wearin' ass had anythin' to do wit' this shit,"
Gator ordered, as the two men left the room.

"Yeah, I felt that way when I met him at Belle Isle last
night. It's somethin' about them New York niggas that make me
uncomfortable."

"I hate them funny talkin' muthafuckas too. That's why we
gotta find out if he had anythin' to do wit' this shit."

"Aight, I'm on it." Deluxe walked over to the window to
see if he could see Myth or Kane in the parking lot. He wanted to
know if they were celebrating or some shit.

"Now I gotta recoup and get that fuckin' Greek piece of shit
his money before I have to deal wit' him too," Gator said to his
nephew, as he rubbed his forehead to relieve the growing tension.

Concerned about what was about to go down, Deluxe
asked, "So what's the plan, 'cause that's a lot of dope and cheese
that we gotta get back."

"Shit, the only plan is to find out if that nigga had any in-
volvement, so I can get my shit back ASAP. I'm gonna rent you a
car, so that faggot won't realize you tailin' him. Oh, and it won't
hurt to go talk to a few fiends that hang outside the dope house.
I'm sure one of them saw or heard somethin'."

"Bet."

Gator cracked his knuckles. "Nephew I'm sure I don't

have to tell you this, but don't fuck this up, and just for future ref-

erences, don't ever double cross me. That way Momma Ruth don't

ever have to plan yo' funeral."

Deluxe looked at his uncle in a bit of disbelief because he

couldn't believe that after what he'd done to Hughes the night be-

fore, Gator would somehow doubt his loyalty.

"Unc, I know it's not easy in this line of work, but you can

trust me."

Well that's the problem, Nephew. I don't trust anyone. Not

even myself.

CHAPTER 6

"This muthafucka can't be trusted," Deluxe said to himself, while he watched Kane from across the street of Gator's dope house in a small, grey Hyundai Accent rental. A car he wouldn't have normally liked to be joy riding in, but under the circumstances, it was perfect for an undercover gig. Deluxe shook his head. He couldn't believe how Kane stood in front of the house flirting with two girls like he didn't have a care in the world, instead of trying to recover his uncle's money.

If he know the spot just got hit why the fuck would his ass be out here rappin' to some potential dope fiends. He seems far from concerned. This shit just don't add up. Everything inside Deluxe told him that the hit was an inside job, and he was damn sure going to find out. There was only one question in his mind that puzzled him. Was Myth involved somehow?

Even though Myth and Gator were best friends and partners in the drug game, everyone knew that sometimes the game turned friends into enemies. Besides, being that Myth had to play the role of sidekick to Gator, Deluxe wasn't sure if that sat too well with him, especially since the two men and his father had started the operation together.

"If Kane is behind this robbery, Myth's loyalty will definitely be tested," Deluxe said to himself as a white Yukon Denali pulled up.

I wonder if that's the same Denali that crack head said he seen leavin' the spot this morning? Deluxe pondered to himself as he spat out shells from the sunflower seeds he continued to pop into his mouth. Deluxe had picked up the crack head two blocks from the dope house a few hours earlier, and after giving him ten dollars, the fiend instantly starting singing like a canary. For an extra five dollar bill, he probably would've told Deluxe where Osama Bin Laden was because crack heads knew and saw everything.

Watching intently now, he saw Kane brush the women off, then hop into the passenger seat of the truck before giving some dap to the driver, who ironically wore the same New York Yankees hat that Kane always sported.

"Yeah, this shit definitely don't look right," Deluxe added. "I mean this nigga ain't even lookin' around to see if the spot is secure or nothin'."

As the white SUV drove off, Deluxe took out his cell phone

and quickly dialed a number. It seemed like forever before Gator finally answered. "Yo, Unc where you at? I got some info for you!" Deluxe asked pulling off. He made sure to follow at a reasonable distance.

"I'm still at the office. I hope you got some good news to tell me."

"I'on know if it's good news or not, but I got some news none the less."

"When can you get here?"

"Well, I'm followin' up on a lead right now, but what I can tell you is that it looks like an inside job."

"Word? An inside job, huh? From who?"

"Kane."

"I knew that shit!" Gator yelled into the phone. "His bitch-ass gonna pay for this. Where you at?"

"Right now I'm just tryin' to see where this nigga goin' cause he's on the move."

"See, that muthafucka didn't even call to tell me he was leavin' the spot or nothin'. I need to call Myth."

"You want me to handle him?" Deluxe asked.

"No, be cool. I got an even better plan for that muthfucka," Gator replied angrily, before they hung up the phone with each other.

Deluxe continued to stalk his prey and followed the SUV all the way to Somerset Mall in Troy where they finally decided to stop and park. He drove past the Denali pretending to be looking for a parking spot, then made sure to pick a space that wasn't too far away.

"Now this fool is about to go spend the money he just copped," Deluxe said, putting the car in park.

He watched as Kane and two other dudes jumped out of the truck, and made their way toward the trunk. Not one person studied their surroundings to see if anything looked suspicious. Luckily for Deluxe, Kane was talking extremely loud, which instantly prompted him to roll down his window.

"Yo, B I'ma need y'all to lay low wit' the paper until all this shit blow over," Kane instructed. He pulled out a black duffle bag then handed it to one of his partners.

"Yeah, word son, that's a lot of shit we got," one short dude replied.

"Yeah but check it, that punk-ass Gator got my cuz tryna find out who did the shit, so we straight on that tip, 'cause I don't think he suspects me. Plus, wasn't nobody out at that time but some crack heads anyway, so I ain't trippin. If we gotta lay that nigga Gator down, then so be it. Once this blow over, we can flip the shit up top wit' my man in the Bronx," Kane boasted.

Why the fuck is he talking so loud? He lettin' the whole world in on the shit, Deluxe thought to himself. *I can't believe Unc would let this dumb-ass nigga in the fam like that. He must be slippin' or somethin'.*

The short dude smiled. "A'ight just break me off wit' my cut duke."

"Look, didn't I just say don't go around bein' flashy? These Detroit niggas can spot a out of town dude from a mile away, so you can't be drawin' no unwanted attention. It's twenty-five large in the bag right now. I'ma hold on to rest until I know y'all niggas followin' the rules," Kane instructed.

"Cool, I'm out son," the short dude replied, giving Kane a pound. He picked up the duffle bag and with the other guy in tow, both men walked to a black cherry Cadillac STS that was conveniently parked a few spaces down. Once again, nobody even looked around to see if they'd been followed. Seconds later, they drove off.

Deluxe shook his head as his eyes returned back to Kane, who by then had jumped back into the Denali, and pulled off as well. This time he noticed that the Cadillac had New Jersey tags.

So that cock sucker really was in on it! I'm gonna enjoy killin' that nigga, a furious Deluxe reasoned to himself as he rolled the window back up and started the car. He couldn't wait to let

Gator know that it was time to handle business.

• •

It took the now steaming assassin almost a half an hour to reach his uncle's office. Even though Deluxe was normally a cool laid back dude, he'd grown cold, callus, and extremely temperamental since joining the Corps. When Deluxe finally arrived, Gator was already on his fifth shot of Hennessy. He looked at Deluxe with glassy eyes as his nephew approached his desk.

"So, what you got for me?"

"Kane was definitely the one who hit the spot. I followed his ass to the parkin' lot at Somerset Mall. He handed these other two New York niggas a duffle bag full of cash. I even overheard the dumb muthafucka braggin' about pullin' the hit off."

Gator was beyond furious. "I need to taste that nigga's blood!" His fist furiously pounded the desk.

"I agree…he needs to be dealt wit' immediately. Just say the word."

"When I talked to Myth he was still takin' up for his bitch-ass," Gator informed. "Did you find out how the shit all went down?"

"Yeah, I talked to this crack head, who was more than willin' to give up the goods on what happened. He said that around three somethin' he went to the spot to cop when this Yukon Denali pulled up with two dudes wearin' red bandannas around their faces. The funny thing is he said when they walked up to the door they knocked like a secret code before kickin' the door in."

"So Kane would know them by the knock, huh?" Gator questioned.

"Exactly, but get this, the crack head said when he saw Kane get in the truck wit' the dudes, it didn't look like he was forced."

"How he know it was Kane?"

"He said the nigga smiled all the way out the house showin' those dumb-ass gold teeth in his mouth."

"I want that muthafucka dead, right fuckin now!"

"Well look, I overheard Kane tellin' his punk-ass crew to lay low until this shit blows over. He gave one of 'em twenty-five grand and told him that he was keepin' the rest 'til they can follow his rules," Deluxe explained to Gator, who was oozing with anger by this time.

"I want everyone involved dead, and if need be, they families too," Gator replied, in a stern voice as he looked callously at his enforcer.

"Yeah remember that funny colored STS, we saw at Belle Isle the other night, well they the dudes who were wit' him, so it's all comin' together. They were probably clockin' us that night. I'm more than sure them dumb-ass fools will go back to the island. It ain't no way they gonna do what Kane said and lay low. You want me to handle them first or Kane?"

"You handle them New York niggas. I got a better idea for Kane. I want Myth to be the one who puts a bullet in that bitches head and right in front of me."

"Yo, Unc I got just one question though, if this shit happened at three somethin', why did it take Myth so long to call and tell you about it? He said it happened around five?"

"I'on know, but I'ma find the fuck out!"

After talking to Gator a few more minutes, Deluxe jumped back in the rental and thought about his game plan all the way to his next destination. Even though he'd gone into the military, he still had a crew of soldiers that he fucked with whenever he was in town. They were former Special Forces in the Army, and were always useful with the families past hits, so he needed to get them on board immediately. Although he was sure the job could've been pulled off solo, he felt the need to make this hit extra special.

• • • • • • • • • • • • • • • • • • •

Deluxe met up with his heavy hitters in the parking lot of Fish Bones restaurant a few hours later to go over the game plan. After tying up a few last minute details, they all jumped in their cars on the way to Belle Isle. Deluxe rode solo while the goons rode in a black Escalade, no rims or anything special, just stock. To play it safe from the cops, he also had two shiesty twins from the hood following the crew a few cars behind in an identical truck. That way if anyone said they saw any sparks flying from a black Escalade the one with the girls could be their decoy. The twins were known for being just as ruthless as men, who fucked for a buck and would kill for much less.

It was around 12:45 a.m., when he noticed the black cherry Cadillac turning onto the island. Ready to make things happen like Queen Latifah and Jada Pinkett did in the movie *Set It Off*, Deluxe called the twins on a disposable Trac phone and told them that he'd spotted the car. Within minutes, the ladies had flagged the STS down and convinced the New York dudes to pull over. Even though the girls were straight out of the projects, their bodies were sick, especially their asses, which clapped every time they took a step.

With only one way in and out the island, the plan was for the twins to get the marks to leave the popular hot spot and follow them to a hotel for a ménage a trois. This way when shit went down, Deluxe didn't have to worry about fleeing the scene in such a congested area.

Five minutes later, one of the twins patted her chest signaling that the plan was in action.

Deluxe smiled. "I knew those idiots would take the bait." He used the Trac phone to call a member of the goon squad. "We straight. Go ahead and roll to the spot. I'll be right behind the girls."

Deluxe had instructed the team of ready killers to park at the Shell gas station on Jefferson Avenue and wait for the girls to pass with the STS following. Deluxe's job was to play clean up and ensure that no one was left breathing.

Deluxe's anticipation was too much to control as he watched the girls jump into the Escalade and head off the island, with the New Yorkers following close behind. As he pulled off himself, he wanted to call Gator to tell him what was about to go down, but quickly changed his mind. He thought he'd relay the good news once the plan had been executed. Tonight, a clear message would be sent to the city.

Ten minutes later, he used the Trac phone again. "Stone, get ready, they about to pass by the gas station," he bellowed to the lead enforcer, who was waiting anxiously for the hit to happen.

"Aight we got the heat ready."

"Remember to get rid of yo' phone once this shit is done."

"Bet."

Deluxe switched lanes and slowed down so that he could get a better view of the massacre that was about to take place. The black Escalade that held the team of street sweepers had turned onto the main strip and sped up close to the Cadillac. That's when he saw the windows come down and the sparks fly. The Escalade with the girls in it sped off while the STS swerved out of control, hitting a wooden fence head on. The car stopped immediately. Deluxe pulled up on the driver's side and jumped out with his Glock drawn. Walking up to the window, he quickly pulled on the door handle, which opened with ease and eagerly dumped two bullets into the driver's head who was already slumped over. Next, he moved with ease and opened fire on the passenger, aiming directly for his head. Deluxe's aim was on point as always.

"Y'all picked the wrong nigga to cross!" Deluxe ruthlessly yelled, as he turned around and jumped back into the rental and sped off. Once he was several miles away from the crime scene, the assassin pulled out the temporary phone and called Gator. When he answered, Deluxe displayed a slight grin.

"It's done," he said in an assuring tone.

"That's what's up. Now make your way over to Molly and Molly's on Woodward Ave," Gator commanded, before hanging up the phone.

• •

Waiting for Deluxe to show up so that his orders of street justice could be carried out, Gator sat in the restaurant parking lot on his Suzuki Hayabusa motorcycle in an all black riding jacket with a giant "G" on the back, his black Prada shades, and a Desert Eagle, nicknamed Death, stuffed in the waist of his pants. On a mission to show why the streets of Detroit belonged to him, Gator was ready for war and the casualties that came with it.

It's time for Kane's bitch- ass to be dealt wit', Gator thought to himself. *And as far as I'm concerned Myth can get it too if he has a problem wit' killin' his cousin, 'cause don't nobody fuck wit' my money.* Gator continued to think, becoming angrier by the second, when Deluxe finally showed up.

"All of 'em dead?" Gator asked, as Deluxe stepped out the car.

"Yep. I put two in them niggas heads personally after my enforcers laid they ass down."

"Good, let's see how Myth reacts when he gets here, and I tell him he has to kill Kane."

"You think he was in on it too?"

Gator shook his head. "Nah, Myth wouldn't do that. At least for his sake, I hope not."

CHAPTER 7

Deluxe and Gator sat gobbling down an order of fried chicken wings and shrimp when Myth walked into the restaurant and sat down at the table.

Each man exchanged half-hearted pounds before Gator stared at his best friend with a tight clenched jaw.

"I found out who stole my shit, and I want you to handle them, tonight!" Gator demanded, while licking the grease off his fingers.

"No doubt, they stole from both of us. My money was tied up in that shit too," Myth replied. "Who is it?"

Without batting an eye Gator replied, "Yo' piece of shit cousin."

Myth was speechless for a moment. "Umm…You can't be serious. You playing right?"

"Nigga, don't it look like I'm serious!" Gator yelled, as a small piece of chicken flew out his mouth. "I'm so serious that I want you to kill his ass in front of me since you brought that muthafucka to the team! Blood or no blood there's only *one blood* in this is business and it's the color of money!"

Deluxe eyed Gator and Myth as the two warriors stared at each other. The tension was beyond thick before Myth finally decided to speak up again.

"So, how do you know it was Kane? I mean I can vouch for my cousin. He good people," Myth explained.

"Well apparently he ain't too good," Gator responded. "I know he was involved because Deluxe been followin' his shady-ass all day. He actually saw Kane hand over a bag of my fuckin' money to some other niggas!"

The expression Myth gave to Deluxe said that he wanted some sort of confirmation.

"Don't be lookin' at my nephew like he lyin' or some shit!" Gator demanded.

Deluxe was about to give the details to Myth when his cell phone rung. Ignoring it at first, the phone continued to ring, until Gator went off.

"Nigga answer the fuckin' phone, or turn the shit off so we can continue wit' business."

Taking Gator's first suggestion, Deluxe pulled out his razor cell phone, never looking at the caller ID. "Yeah," he answered in an aggravated tone.

"Now I know you weren't just gonna come into town without trying to see me were you?" the sweet seductive voice asked, on the other end of the phone.

Damn, I knew I shouldn't have answered this shit, Deluxe thought before responding. "Naa, I just been busy takin' care of some business. How did you find out that I was here?"

"Kandi's jealous-ass told me that she saw you, Gator and Myth at Belle Isle. I thought we were better than that, or maybe I just don't mean anything to you anymore?"

Deluxe felt somewhat guilty about the way the Rachelle put things in perspective because normally he did call her when he got into town, but he couldn't show any weakness in front of Myth and Gator. He stood up and walked a few feet away from the table. "Come on, don't act like that. I said I been busy. Look we can …"

Before he could get the last sentence out, that soft tempting voice interrupted him. "Jayson look, I need…I need to see you. I'm horny as hell."

Hearing the sexiness in Rachelle's voice instantly made Deluxe's dick hard. At that point, he had to make the time to see her. He also had to hurry up and get her off the phone before Gator started yelling again. "Okay, how about breakfast tomorrow morning around 10:00 a.m. at the Pancake House on 10 Mile and Evergreen?"

"I wouldn't miss it," Rachelle cooed. "You still love me?"

Why is she asking me that shit, he pondered before replying, "Look, I'll see you in the morning. I gotta go."

After hanging up the phone Deluxe sat back down at the table and thought about the incredible sex he and Rachelle always had. He loved the way her pussy wrapped around his manhood like a glove. He was starting to get deeper into his thoughts when Myth's and Gator's loud arguing interrupted him.

"I guess this puts us at odds then, because I ain't killin' my cousin!" Myth replied, with cockiness to his voice.

Not puzzled by Myth's response, Gator issued his ultimatum. "Fuck what you talkin', either you deal wit' his bitch-ass or else. Business is business."

Myth shook his head like he could care less.

"Now you know you my nigga for life. I mean shit, I'm your son's Godfather, so it's puzzlin' to me how you could be so careless to bring a disloyal fuck like Kane to my team," Gator continued.

"He ain't fuckin' disloyal," Myth stated, still defending his cousin.

Gator was disappointed that Myth still didn't believe Kane was grimey, and had violated the family's number one rule. "Well then it is what it is and this is business. That fuckin' cousin of yours robbed me of my shit. Now I want him dealt wit'!" Gator commanded.

Myth knew at that moment it would be the last night he and Gator would be in business together or maybe even alive at the same time. "Like you said, it is what it is," Myth replied, before standing up and walking out of the restaurant.

Gator knew that it wouldn't be easy laying down the law to his best friend, especially after all of the shit they'd done together coming up in the game. Now all the years of getting money to-gether, fucking bitches coast to coast, and building a dynasty, was all about to come to an end. But everyone who decides to play the game of the streets knew that there were certain rules that couldn't be broken. Disloyalty wasn't one of them.

"You know what you gotta do now?" Gator asked, looking at Deluxe. "Let's get Kane first, and deal wit' Myth later."

Replying with callousness in his voice, Deluxe replied, "One blood," signifying his loyalty to the cause.

CHAPTER 8

The sound of the piercing alarm startled Deluxe the next morning, breaking him out of much needed sleep. *Damn I can't wait to get a full eight hours,* he thought as he attempted to drag himself out of bed. However, with memories of last night's events still fresh in his mind he knew getting eight hours in the near future were highly unlikely. Before his feet could touch the floor his cell phone started ringing.

Deluxe reached over on the night stand and picked it up. "Hello," he answered, in a groggy voice.

"Hey, listen instead of going to the Pancake House, why don't you meet me at my house instead?" Rachelle suggested.

Feeling setup Deluxe sucked his teeth. "I hate it when people change plans at the last minute and shit."

"Why have you been such an asshole lately? Maybe you should stop hanging out with your uncle if you're gonna act like this."

"Rachelle you really startin' to piss me off, so cut the bullshit a'ight."

"Boy, just bring your ass to my house. I wanted to cook for you. I promise you'll like the surprise I have," she exclaimed, before hanging up in his face.

Surprise huh? I wonder what kind of surprise she got for me, he wondered before jumping in the shower to get ready.

• •

On the drive over to Rachelle's house in Oak Park, Deluxe thought about everything that was going down. Normally when he came home, he enjoyed himself. However, this time he was busy spending time looking over his shoulder and wondering if and when shit was going to go wrong. In only two days this military trained killer had bodied three people, and there were even more to come.

"Should I take the Glock in with me? I can't get careless now," Deluxe said to himself, as he pulled into Rachelle's driveway. After contemplating for a few more seconds he decided to take the pistol inside just to be on the safe side. He didn't have time to take any chances. After getting out the car, he walked up a small flight of stairs to the door, but before he could press the doorbell, Rachelle greeted him wearing a hot pink, satin flyaway baby doll top, with the matching thong panties from Victoria's Secret.

"Are you just gonna stand there with your mouth open or

are you gonna come in?" she asked. She licked her lips seductively.

Smiling as he closed the door behind him, Deluxe replied, "Damn girl you looking good. I see you been taking care of yourself," he said, while grabbing the front of his pants to massage his rising dick.

Her lingerie revealed an ass like one that you would find in the eye candy section of XXL Magazine. Even though they were both a little older now, nothing much had changed about her. Rachelle was still thick as hell with a pair of the sexiest lips that Deluxe had ever seen. He began to think back to when they were in Jr. High. Even back then her body was ridiculous. She was shorter than most of the girls in their class, about 5'1', but she was thick and as a cheerleader for the basketball team her legs were amazing. Every nigga in the school used to try and holla at her. Her cocoa brown complexion and long jet-black hair made her the pick of the litter.

"So what's the surprise?" he asked, as Rachelle led him by the hand down the hall to a bedroom that had scented candles lit, and Pleasure & Pain by 112 playing softly in the background.

"This," she whispered, while kissing Deluxe on the ear.

So much for breakfast, he thought.

Pushing him to the bed, Rachelle stood over her part time

lover taking off each piece of lingerie illuminating her perfectly sculpted abs and a pair of the most succulent voluptuous breasts Deluxe had ever seen. Doing a sexy dance as she stood on the bed, he could see Rachelle's nipples begin to stand at attention. She commanded her lover to take off his clothes, as she bent over in front of an aroused Deluxe providing a full view of her flawlessly manicured pussy, which was beginning to pulsate. Never taking his eyes off her kitty, he quickly took off his clothes and exposed a throbbing penis which was now beginning to swell with anticipation of what was about to go down. Without warning, Rachelle grabbed the shaft of his manhood and began to suck it like it was a fruit filled lollipop. Not wanting to cum too soon, Deluxe grabbed Rachelle and flipped her over onto her stomach. Quickly getting on all fours, she arched her back slightly waiting for Deluxe to fuck her in the doggy-style position. Slowly, he entered her pool of passion causing Rachelle to let out a soft moan. He enjoyed the sound of his balls as they began to slap against her ass once he found the perfect rhythm. When Rachelle's moans became louder, Deluxe decided to dig deeper and sped up the tempo.

"You like this dick?" Deluxe asked, as his thrusts became even harder.

"Ye...s...," she managed to get out. However, despite his rapid strokes, Rachelle placed her finger directly on her throbbing clit, then began to move it in a circular motion.

Seeing how freaky she always got when they had sex, Deluxe could feel himself about to explode. He pounded away at her pussy, until the strong surge of sperm traveled from his testicles up to his shaft. He pulled out immediately, spitting out a large amount of cum onto Rachelle's chest.

The two of them ended up making love, several more times that day until the 112 CD repeated itself and all the candles had burned out. After the marathon love making session they both held on to each other.

"Jayson?" Rachelle asked, while her head continued to lie on Deluxe's muscular chest.

"What's up?"

"Can I ask you something? And you promise to tell me the truth."

Expecting her question to be about the two of them, he replied, "Of course."

"Are you working with your uncle Gator in that mess that's been going on around the city?"

He sat up in the bed. "Why you askin' me somethin' like that?"

"Because I know what Gator's into, and I don't want to see you get caught up in that. You have too much to live for. Besides, he's just not a good influence."

Deluxe was becoming a bit agitated at her insistence to know. "Why do you even care? What I do with my uncle is none of yo' business."

"So, you can fuck me, but I can't ask you any questions?"

Deluxe stared at Rachelle. "So that's why you threw yo' pussy on me today? To get in my damn business?"

Refusing to look Deluxe in the eyes, Rachelle let out a sigh. "Kandi told me that when she saw y'all, it looked like they were congratulating you on something serious. I just don't want you caught up in the bullshit that's going on around here. You don't have to get defensive, I was just asking."

Not wanting to ruin the moment they'd just shared, Deluxe pulled her closer to him and while looking her in the eyes said, "No, I'm not doing anything with my uncle Gator. I'm just in town to take care of some business and then I'm going back to North Carolina."

He felt sort of guilty about the blatant lie he'd just told. After the commitment he'd made to his uncle, he didn't have any plans to go back at all.

"I just don't want to see anything happen to you baby. We may not be in a relationship anymore, but I still care about you," Rachelle admitted, as she kissed him on his chest. It wasn't long before she worked her way down and placed Deluxe's rising penis in her mouth again.

• •

Later that night, Deluxe searched around the city like a blood hound looking for Kane or anyone who even remotely looked like him. It was important that he found the double crossing dude before Myth got to him first, so the family's plan of execution could be carried out. Using some of their informants in the streets, Gator had put a price on Kane's head for anyone that led him to his whereabouts. With $50,000 at stake, they both knew it wouldn't take long. After looking at the caller ID on his cell phone, Deluxe quickly answered.

"What up Unc?"

"The streets already talkin' Nephew," Gator said excitedly. "Somebody just called me and said that Kane is at Plan B. Word is that he was up in there last night too, poppin' bottles and makin' it rain up in the VIP."

"That fool is spendin' your cheese like it's his," Deluxe replied in a malicious tone.

"Yeah, well like Biggie said, somebody's got to die."

"How you wanna handle this, especially if Myth is up in there with him? Oh, wait a minute, what about Jimmy the Greek. What if he's there? You know his office is in the same VIP area."

"I heard that him and his bitch, Sonny is out of town at some weddin'," Gator replied. "And as far as Myth and Kane goes, if they both spendin' my bread, they both gotta go!"

"Good, now I can stop ridin' around lookin' for his ass."

"Let's take the rental to the spot, so come pick me up from the crib. I'll be ready when you get here."

Deluxe laughed. "Are you sure you wanna drive around in this bullshit?" he asked. "I know you used to the finer things in life."

"Shit, everybody in the whole city of Detroit knows all my fuckin' whips, so my shit can't be seen. Besides, right now I'm so anxious to get this muthafucka my dick is hard, so I'll ride over there in a damn four wheeler if I have to."

Deluxe laughed again. "Well everybody in Detroit also knows who you are. Maybe you should sit this one out."

"And miss this nigga dyin' for the shit he did? Absolutely not. Trust me, I got a plan, just come pick me up."

CHAPTER 9

Pulling up to the valet at the club forty minutes later, Gator motioned for the parking valet over to the window.

When the older man walked over, Gator rolled down the window and stuck his hand out. "Listen, here's $500. Park my shit around the back by the exit and leave it runnin' B," he said in his best New York accent.

The valet looked at Gator like he was crazy, and had a reason. Both men had on shiny fake gold teeth, huge sunglasses and New York Yankees hats pulled down so low, they could barely see themselves. Gator had also traded in his signature alligator shoes for a new pair of crisp Nike Air Force Ones.

"Yeah, you heard right son. Once you park it, I need you to stay wit' my shit. Can you handle that?" Gator asked.

Although the parking attendant still seemed suspicious, he shook his head up and down.

"Word. Oh, and you didn't see the person drivin' this car if someone asks B, especially if you wanna keep your life son."

The attendant's response was just another head nod.

"You got the silencer I gave you for that piece?" Gator asked Deluxe, as they both exited the Hyundai.

"Yeah, that was a good idea. We don't need the canon drawin' more attention than this dude's dead body."

"I know, so let's go handle this shit Nephew and get the fuck up outta here."

When they walked into the club, several women immediately flocked to them thinking they had money. Not wanting to draw attention to the slaughter that was about to take place, Gator stopped by the bar and bought a couple of bottles of champagne, and few shots of Patrón for the scandalous women who were on their coat tails. Before they made their way to the VIP, Deluxe grabbed one of the waitresses and told her to take a bottle of Cristal that he'd just bought to a dude named Kane in the VIP.

"If he asked who sent it Ma, tell him God," Deluxe continued, is his fake accent slipping her the $100 bill. With that, she was off.

"Money always talks in the fuckin' D," Gator said, with a huge smile.

● ● ● ● ● ● ● ● ● ● ● ● ● ● ● ● ● ● ●

"Why the fuck is this nigga not answerin' the phone?" Myth asked himself as he closed his phone. He'd been calling Kane since the meeting between him and Gator didn't go so well, but his cousin still hadn't returned any of his calls.

I gotta get him back to New York before Gator finds him. Where the fuck can he be? I don' looked everywhere for his ass, he thought.

Becoming discouraged about not being able to reach Kane, Myth called his cell phone again, but this time decided to leave a message on his voicemail. "Look nigga you need to call me back. I need you to go back up top and lay low for a minute until we can figure out what to do about this bullshit," Myth said hanging up the phone.

Ain't nobody seen him at none of the spots, and I can't find none of his bitches either, so there's only one place left to check, Plan B, Myth reasoned as he decided to go to the club and see if his cousin was there.

•••••••••••••••••••••

Before Deluxe and Gator made their way upstairs to the VIP, Gator decided that all the attention they were getting from the gold diggers in the club was actually a good plan, so to divert the attention away from them, he pulled out a stack and made it rain to club hit, *'Independent'* by Webbie. As the money hungry bitches started fighting for the money, Deluxe and Gator walked into the VIP to see Kane snorting lines of coke and getting a lap dance at the same time.

"So, this is what my money's buyin', huh nigga?" Gator asked, removing his disguise. He wanted Kane to know who was about to put his ass to sleep. He stared maliciously at the trader, who was still in a daze from the line of coke he'd just snorted.

"Yo B, I was …"

Before Kane could reply Gator yelled, "Shut the fuck up before I twist yo' ass myself. I shoulda shot yo' bitch-ass the other day!" Yelling to the strippers in the room, Gator told them, "Get the fuck out!"

Trying to man up, or use her as a bullet proof vest, Kane looked at the girl on his lap, who was about to get up. "Naa Ma, you stay yo' ass right here, fuck these clown ass niggas!"

Hearing enough, Gator slapped the high yellow broad causing her to fall to the floor. Sobbing uncontrollably, she looked up at Gator with a stream of blood running out of her mouth and a handprint across the right side of her cheek. Before Kane could jump up off the couch, Gator looked at Deluxe, "Mark this muthafucka," he ordered, in a cold voice.

Without saying a word, the certified killer took the Glock out his waist and pointed it directly at Kane's face. Staring down the barrel, Kane threw his hands up. Stuttering, he tried his best to get the words out, "Wai…"

Before he could finish screaming the word wait to plead his

case, Deluxe squeezed the trigger catching him in the forehead. Brain matter blew all over the thick stripper who was now in the fetal position on the floor screaming.

"Please…no…no don't kill me, I got two kids at home. Please don't kill me," she repeated over and over.

Laughing uncontrollably, Gator grabbed the girl by her hair. "If you say anything to anyone, I'll have those kids you were just talkin' about raped right in front of you, and when that's done, I'll have them muthafuckas killed," Gator whispered.

The stripper instantly started crying even louder.

"Remember, you didn't see nothin', and you don't know nothin' either bitch," Deluxe added, before both men walked out.

• •

Pulling into the parking lot of the club and seeing the line of police cars, and the paramedics, Myth fears that the dead body being brought out on the gurney was his cousin. He quickly jumped out of his car, then made an attempt to make it toward the body. However, the police crime scene tape wouldn't allow him to get any further.

"I need to get through, I think that may be someone I know!" he yelled.

Instantly he got the attention of a detective who was standing nearby. "So, you're saying that you might know the gentleman who was murdered here tonight?" he asked.

"Well, I think so, but I'm not sure. What was his name?"

The detective's face lit up. "Wow, you're the first person tonight who's even willing to talk to us in public. Hey listen…why don't you come down to the station, so we could ask you a few questions."

Myth knew how this was going to work. In order for him to find out if Kane was under the sheet, he had to seem as cooperative as possible. "Officer…"

"No, Detective. Detective Bridges."

"Oh, sorry Detective Bridges. I'll be happy to come down, but I need to know who was murdered. If I know him, I need to contact his mother," Myth lied with a straight face.

The detective sighed. "Look, normally I wouldn't do this, but since you're willing to help us out here, I'll help you." Detective Bridges looked at his little notepad. "The driver's license we found on the victim says his name was Erick Foster, but a few people in the club said he went by the name Kane. Does that ring a bell?"

Myth's heart almost stopped. He couldn't believe Gator had gotten to him before he could.

"Sir, does that name ring a bell?" Detective Hughes repeated.

Myth had to hold his composure. "Actually sir, it doesn't. I've been lookin' for my friend all night, and I was hoping that wasn't him. Sorry to interrupt you." Myth turned around and quickly walked away.

The detective seemed beyond frustrated. "So are you still willing to come to the station?"

Myth never looked back or responded.

Once he was back inside his car, Myth pulled out his cell phone and dialed a series of numbers. *I bet Gator's ass won't expect this one. Payback is a bitch.*

"We need to meet, just me and you," he said to the person on the other end.

"I knew you would come around."

CHAPTER 10

"Here's a recent picture, can you handle this project?" Myth inquired, as he put his plan for revenge in motion.

"Of course I can. Have I ever let you down before?"

"You get five stacks up front and the remainin' five when it's all over."

She counted the money before placing the new found wealth in her new Gucci purse. "So, when do you want all this to happen?" Kandi asked, with a sinister smirk on her face.

"The sooner the better."

"Consider it done," Kandi replied, before standing up to leave the Fish Bones restaurant. Myth watched the beautiful seductress as she walked toward the door in her skin tight Rock & Republic jeans and low cut shirt then smiled.

The high heeled shoes made her look taller than her normal 5'3' frame, and the black Chanel eyeglasses that eloquently graced her impeccable caramel face gave her the look of a school teacher who was ready to paddle any student who'd misbehaved in class.

Myth knew that no one would see his plan coming. Ever

since he'd seen his cousin being taken out on a gurney, he'd made it his mission to bring down Gator and prove to everyone, who the real king of Detroit was.

Walking to her silver metallic Grand Prix, Kandi pulled out the Blackberry from her purse to make a call. "Hey, I got the info. This should be a easy-ass job."

"You get the down payment?" the raspy voiced man asked from the other end of the phone.

"Of course. I don't fuck or work for free," she remarked, before pressing the end button on her phone.

Pulling the picture out of her purse, Kandi stared at the image and began to think about the task at hand. She laughed to herself at the thought of what was about to go down. She'd always used her body and exotic looks for crazy things before, but never for a mission like this.

Kandi displayed a slight grin before dialing another number on her phone. As she waited for someone to answer, the grin turned into a huge smile when thoughts of her big payday floated around her head.

"Thanks for calling Stevens Realty."

"Hello, may I speak with a Ms. Mylani Stevens," Kandi said.

"Yes, this is Mylani, how may I help you?"

"Hi Mylani, my name is Kiyanna Larsen and I'm in the market for a condo. I received one of your business cards from a friend of mine who highly recommended you," she replied, hoping to suck Mylani into her trap.

"Okay Ms. Larsen, or is it Mrs. Larsen?"

Laughing at the question Kandi replied, "It's Ms. but you can just call me Kiyanna."

"Alright Kiyanna. Any particular areas you're interested in?"

"Definitely the downtown area because price is not a option," Kandi replied, trying her best to sound like she had money.

Mylani chuckled. She'd heard that line more times than she could remember. "Well, you're in luck. I happen to have a couple of condos in the financial district of downtown that have just come up on the market. I have an opening in my schedule today around 5:00 p.m. if you're available to meet with me so that I can show you these fabulous properties."

"Five is perfect. Where's your office?"

After Mylani gave her the address, Kandi smiled. *This shit may be easier than I thought. All I have to do is get her to trust me and she won't know what hit her.*

Excited about the possibility of selling one of the hottest condo's in the city, Mylani said, "I look forward to seeing you

Kiyanna."

"Great, I look forward to seeing you as well," Kandi replied before hanging up. Speeding down the highway, she turned up, 50 Cent's '*I Get Money,*' which at the moment should've been her theme song. "This shit about to get me paid. Fuck stripping if I can do this."

Not knowing if she would be able to make dinner, Mylani called Gator to let him know that she may not be home by her usual 6:00 p.m. time. When he didn't answer the phone, she decided to leave a message.

"Hey baby. Listen, I just talked to a new client who wants me to take her to see those new condo's downtown. I think I'm gonna take her to the Woodyard Avenue building, the one across from Campus Park. You remember the building I showed you while we were driving the other day? Anyway, I may be a little late coming home, so just wanted you to know. Oh, by the way I bought you a card, but don't open it until I get there. I want to see the look on your face, when you read it. Love you."

● ●

Wearing a short red dress, that instantly read stripper, Kandi stood in the lobby of Mylani's downtown office awaiting the arrival of the woman she'd only seen on a picture. Seconds later the elevator door chimed, and out walked a beautiful woman dressed in a St. John suit, open toed Jimmy Choo shoes, a Louis Vuitton handbag from her confident collection and her lengthy hair pulled up in a high ponytail. As Mylani walked toward Kandi she couldn't help but to observe her exotic beauty from head to toe.

Damn she's more beautiful than I thought she would be; but if she wants to keep those good looks she better do what the fuck I tell her.

"Hi you must be Kiyanna?" Mylani remarked, revealing a set of flawlessly white teeth.

She extended her hand to greet Kandi, who had a slight smirk on her face.

"And you must be Mylani, so nice to meet you," the venomous seductress replied, as she shook her mark's hand.

"Can I get you anything before we go take a look at the condo?" Mylani wanted to have her potential client feel at ease.

"No thank you, but thanks for asking."

"Okay well follow me, we can take my car. That way you don't have to use any of your gas."

"Girl, I appreciate that, but I can drive. Trust me. I'm not hurting for money," Kandi replied still playing the part of a baller.

"Oh no, I insist. I don't like my clients to worrying about driving."

As they made their way to the garage, Kandi intently

watched Mylani's ass move from side to side in the pencil skirt that wrapped firmly around her ass like a baseball glove. *Too bad fucking her is not part of the deal. I bet her pussy is just as sweet as those succulent lips look on her face,* she thought.

Still fantasizing about Mylani's assets, Kandi didn't even hear her ask if she was new to the area.

"Huh? Oh yeah, I just moved here from Lansing. My job transferred me about a month ago," she replied, trying to snap from her daze.

"So, you've been renting all this time or staying with family?"

In a playful girlish laugh Kandi replied, "Actually, I've been living out of my suitcase in a hotel. I refuse to stay with any of my sorry-ass cousins around the city."

Sharing a laugh about the comment Mylani smiled as they approached her BMW.

"I see you have exquisite taste when it comes to cars," Kandi remarked, as Mylani activated the alarm and opened up the passenger side door.

For some reason Mylani was slightly embarrassed by Kandi's comment. "Yeah, my man bought it for me as a birthday gift."

Kandi was beyond jealous. "It must be nice to drive a car

like this." Resting her plump ass on the butter soft leather seats, she still wondered why Mylani was the mark and not Gator's paid-ass. Things were just not adding up.

In the short time it took to drive to the downtown condos, the two women talked and laughed like high school girls forming an instant bond that would prove to be treacherous in the near future. Continuing to formulate her plan, Kandi inquired about the local hot spots for happy hour, the finest places to dine, and of course the most immaculate places to unwind such as the nearest and best spa the city. Feeling like they were kindred souls from the same sorority, Mylani suggested that Kandi join her for a day of shopping and pampering at the spa once the settlement on her brand new house occurred. Realizing that she was quickly gaining her trust, Kandi accepted her offer as they pulled up in front up to the twenty-five story building and into the adjoining parking lot.

Once the two ladies stepped out of the car, Kandi felt important when they walked inside the grand lobby with it's granite walls, marble floors and vaulted ceilings. "Wow, this is nice," she said.

"I know, and this is just the lobby," Mylani responded. "Look at the breathtaking floor to ceiling windows."

"Oh, before we go upstairs, I need to take a quick smoke break outside. I know I need to quit, but it's a bad habit."

"No need to explain yourself to me Kiyanna. I'll wait here until you're done."

Kandi turned around and proceeded to walk but stopped. "What floor are we going to because I would prefer something higher?"

Mylani looked sort of confused, but was still polite. The last thing she wanted was to piss off a potential buyer. "Actually this works out because we're going to the twenty-first floor, unit 2103."

"I guess this is my lucky day," Kandi responded, with a cheesy grin as she quickly walked out the lobby doors. Once outside, she walked to the corner of the building and then pulled out her cell phone. It was at the moment, when the adrenaline began to rush through her body. After dialing the number, she paced back and forth until her accomplice finally answered.

"What up?"

"Listen, we downtown at the intersection of Woodyard and Michigan Avenue." Kandi looked at the building until she saw the address. "1001 Woodyard Avenue to be exact. 2103 is the condo number."

"Bet. I'll be there in a minute. Don't take all fuckin' day," the deep voice responded, before hanging up.

"I hate it when that muthafucka act like he running the

show," Kandi said, closing her phone. When she walked back into the building, Mylani was waiting as promised.

"Everything okay?"

Kandi smiled. "Yes, thanks for waiting. I needed that cancer stick."

"Good," Mylani said, walking toward the elevator. After pushing the up arrow, she turned to face Kandi. "This building has concierge services, a state of the art fitness center, dry cleaning services, and much more."

"Sold," Kandi joked.

"Well just wait until you see the condo."

When the elevator door opened, the two ladies stepped inside. During the short ride to the twenty-first floor, Mylani continued to use her best sales pitch, telling Kandi all about the buildings amenities. Seconds later, the elevator door opened again, and the two walked to unit 2103.

"Hopefully this will be your new home," Mylani said, putting the key into the door.

"I hope so. I can't wait to get out that hotel," Kandi lied. When Mylani opened the door to the 1600 sq. foot condo, Kandi's eyes lit up as she walked into the small foyer. *See I need to be living in some shit like this for real.*

Mylani closed the door. "Okay Kiyanna, let me give you a

tour." She placed her Louie Vuitton bag on the floor. "This is a two

bedroom unit, with two and a half bathrooms and two huge walk in

closets, which I'm sure you could use."

Kandi smiled. "Girl of course. I got too many damn

clothes." She walked into the living room, and immediately

stopped in front of the huge windows. The view of downtown De-

troit was beautiful.

"As you can see the condo has lots of character with these

hardwood floors, and the beautiful state of the art kitchen," Mylani

added in her professional real estate voice."

"Yeah, I don't even need to see anymore. How much is it?"

Mylani smiled thinking she didn't even have to put in a lot

of work. "This unit starts at $388,000, but could go up depending

on if you want any upgrades."

"Great, I'll take it."

"Are you sure, you don't want to see anything else?"

Kandi shook her head. "No, this is perfect. We can go back

to your office and start on the paperwork."

"I don't think I've ever had a sell this quickly. You're a

woman who knows what she wants," Mylani stated.

"I know girl, when I want something I jump on it," Kandi

stated, as she secretly hoped her partner in crime would be waiting.

As they approached the front door and opened it, a man

standing about 6 feet tall with an athletic muscular build stood in front of the door and attacked both women. Pushing Kandi to the floor, the brute slapped Mylani across the right side of her face knocking her purse out of her hand. She immediately pleaded for her life.

"Please don't… don't hurt my baby… I'm pregnant!" Mylani yelled.

However, before she could muster the strength to make another plea her face was met with a cloth full of chloroform instantly knocking her unconscious.

"Why the fuck did you push me down?" Kandi questioned, as her partner grabbed Mylani before she could hit the floor.

"To make the shit look good," he replied. "Close the fuckin' door!"

"Look good for who muthafucka? Who cares what this bitch thinks!" Kandi yelled as she stood up. Even though she was mad, once Kandi looked down at Mylani and realized who she'd just kidnapped, hitting the floor was definitely worth it.

• •

With an aching head, a sore face, her mouth gagged and her hands tied behind her back, Mylani woke up a few hours later to find herself stripped naked and laying on the cold hardwood floor of the living room. Strangely, she was still in the condo.

Mylani began to mumble screams through the duct tape that was wrapped around her mouth, which only pissed her kidnappers off.

"Bitch, shut the fuck up before I kill you," Kandi's partner demanded.

Looking at her fine body, the man began to run his hands over her breasts and down her abdomen toward her legs which were shaking hysterically. Before he could get to her pleasure palace he was interrupted by a shove from his accomplice.

"What the fuck are you doing? That's not part of the plan. Let's make the call," Kandi ordered, as she looked at Mylani with a devilish grin on her face. "Did you sleep well?"

Looking up at Kandi with shock, tears began to race down Mylani's face.

Realizing her anguish, Kandi knelt down beside Mylani and whispered in her ear, "It's nothin' personal sweetie, strictly business."

Hanging her head in defeat Mylani prayed to herself hoping that God wouldn't abandon her and that someone would come to her rescue.

If only Gerald knew where I was. Please God help me. I don't know what they're gonna do to me, she prayed in her thoughts as tears continued to cover her swollen face.

Kandi picked up her cell phone and dialed Myth's number. "We have the package, but there's been a change of plans. We want $100,000 cash by nine o'clock or we're killing her ass!"

"Bitch you must be out yo' fuckin' mind. The deal was for her to be kidnapped and then handed to me, not killed!"

"Well nigga the game plan don' changed. You and Gator run Detroit, so I'm sure y'all can afford it."

"Look Kanidi, I ain't givin' yo' money hungry-ass shit other than the ten stacks we already agreed upon!" Myth yelled through the phone.

"Suit yourself nigga, like I said you only have until nine or it's a fucking rap," Kandi barked.

Before Myth could finish yelling, "Bitch," Kandi hung up the phone and threw it on the floor.

"What did the nigga say?" her partner asked.

"That shit he talking don't matter. But what does matter is that muthafucka better come through with $100,000 or lil' miss prissy here is dying." Kandi cut her eyes at Mylani, who was now wondering who the person on the other end of the phone was.

"We might as well have a little fun with our friend here until we hear back from Myth," the ruthless brute said, as he walked toward Mylani.

Looking at her round perky breast and her Brazilian waxed

pussy, Kandi agreed as she began kissing Mylani on the neck. Her moans for help fell on deaf ears as she was unable to escape the clutches of the two evil people that were now groping and fondling her helpless body.

Overcome with fear Mylani almost passed out from the thought of her body being violated as the two assailants took turns sticking their fingers in her pussy. Before long, Kandi's partner, bent Mylani over and violently shoved his large dick deep into her ass, causing her anal walls to tear and bleed as he pumped harder and harder until he erupted inside her. Collapsing onto the floor, Mylani sobbed uncontrollably as the pain took over her body. Taking his now limp dick out of Mylani's open ass, Kandi's partner stood up then wiped the blood and cum off.

"That was some nasty shit, but I loved it," Kandi remarked. She rubbed her hand against Mylani's ass despite her pain. "Now, it's time for me to have some fun."

With the help of her partner, Kandi flipped Mylani on her back, then spread her legs wide open. It wasn't long before Kandi stuck her long thick tongue out and began to devour Mylani's pussy. By this time, Mylani was in so much shock, she just laid there as the brutal rape continued.

As the time drew closer to nine, Kandi called Myth one more time to see if he was prepared to meet her demands. "Time's up. Do we have a deal?" she questioned, as her partner was preparing to put a bullet into Mylani's head.

Aware that his plan was spiraling out of control, Myth attempted to ask for more time, but was interrupted by the sound of two gun shots going off, and then dead air on the phone.

CHAPTER 11

"I swear yo' ass give one hell of a fuckin' blow job," Gator moaned, as one of his groupies wiped her mouth. "My dick is hooked on those nice juicy lips."

Gator had been in a hotel in Madison Heights for most of the evening doing what he was known for, fucking and snorting coke. However, during all this he'd also been calling Mylani every thirty minutes, trying his best to see where she was, but so far he still couldn't get in touch with her. He reached on the nightstand and grabbed his phone for what seemed like the hundredth time.

"Where the fuck she at? It's unlike her to be out this late and not answer her phone," Gator mumbled to himself, as he dialed her cell phone number. When she didn't answer, he tried the house. By this time he was pissed hoping she wasn't cheating on him as well. Again, his call was answered by the house voicemail.

"Where the fuck you at? It's almost 11:00 p.m.! I swear Mylani you better get yo' ass in the house before I get there!" he yelled into the phone.

"Problems at home huh?" the groupie asked.

"I'ma fuck her ass up, that's what I'ma do," he replied, closing his cell phone.

"So, what if she's out doing the same thing you doing?"

Gator looked at the groupie like she was deranged. "Bitch don't you ever come out yo' mouth like that again. Besides. I'm the only one who can do shit like that. My lady know better."

Picking up his phone again, for the first time, Gator decided to check and see if Mylani had left him a voicemail by any chance. However, after checking the message he still had an attitude.

"This shit still don't make sense. Her ass went to show a condo hours ago, and she still ain't home. Why hasn't she called me?" he asked himself out loud.

"She probably out fucking somebody else like you nigga," the groupie butted in.

"Bitch you need to mind yo' damn business. As a matter of fact, get on your fuckin' knees and do yo' job again. All you need to do is worry about this dick."

Gator held his head back as the groupie didn't waste any-time doing what she was told, but a few seconds later, all of that changed when the 11:00 p.m. news top story came through the television's speakers.

"On tonight's top story, police found an African American woman, brutally raped and murdered earlier tonight, inside of a vacant Woodyard Avenue condo. We go live to the scene where Natalie Woods, has the story...Natalie," the first news anchor informed.

Gator immediately sat up and stared at the TV in shock. As soon as he heard the name of the street, his heart felt like it had dropped in the pit of his stomach. He began to play Mylani's message over and over in his head. "Stop!" he yelled to the groupie who was still trying to suck his dick.

"Thanks Carol, in what has been described as a gruesome scene, police were called after neighbors heard several gunshots coming from a Woodyard Avenue condo, which is actually vacant," the news reporter stated, as she pointed to the building. "When officers arrived, they found a woman dead with a gunshot wound to her head and abdomen. Police have identified the body, as Mylani Stevens, a well known and highly respected realtor in the Detroit area. Sources say more than likely Ms. Stevens was actually showing the condo to a potential client, where she was gunned down. Police tell us as of right now there are no suspects. We'll provide more details as they become available. Back to you Carol."

Gator felt like he was about to throw up. He jumped up not wanting to face the reality that the dead woman from the news report was the love of his life. He frantically dialed her cell phone number again. "Come on Mylani baby answer the phone." When she didn't answer, Gator quickly started putting on his clothes.

"What are you doing?" the groupie asked.

"What the fuck does it look like? I gotta go!"

"But how am I supposed to get home?"

Gator wanted to slap the shit out of her for annoying him. "Bitch, I gave you four hundred dollars when we first got here. Figure the shit out!"

After buttoning his shirt, Gator made sure to grab his Desert Eagle and headed straight for the door. However, before he could get all the way out the room, his cell phone starting ringing. It was Momma Ruth.

He knew what the call was about and could barely speak. "Hello."

"Gerald baby, you need to sit down," Momma Ruth suggested.

A single tear ran down Gator's cheek as he walked back toward the bed and sat down. "I already know Momma."

"Oh Gerald, I'm so sorry. Mylani was like a daughter to me."

"Did you see it on the news?"

"Yes, but for some reason Mylani's license must've been registered to my house, so the police called me as soon as they found her body. I was the one who told them to release her name because I want those bastards who did this to be caught."

"Oh, don't worry those muthafucka's will be dealt wit'."

"Gerald Green, don't do anything stupid because that's not going to help the situation. I already buried one son. I don't want to bury another one."

By this time Gator's one tear had turned to many. "Momma, I gotta go."

"Wait baby. There's more." Momma Ruth seemed hesitant to continue as she cleared her throat. "I hate to tell you this, but Mylani was pregnant. She told me yesterday, and had plans on telling you today."

Gator pounded his fist on his leg. "So, that's probably what was on the card she wanted me to read."

Momma Ruth was quiet for a second. "I guess so," she replied in a low tone. Seconds later all she heard was a dial tone. Gator had obviously hung up.

They're only two people who would have enough balls to fuck wit' my girl like this, and I'ma kill both of those muthafuckas and their entire family, Gator thought as he hopped off the bed, and for the second time, headed out the door.

• • • • • • • • • • • • • • • • • • •

"What's good Unc?" Deluxe answered, bringing an end to

the phone calls he'd been ignoring.

Sobbing almost uncontrollably his uncle replied, "Where the fuck have you been? I been callin' yo' ass for almost a hour."

Even though Gator seemed upset, Deluxe still smiled. "Oh, sorry about that. I'm over Rachelle's house, and we were sort of busy if you know what I mean." He knew his uncle would understand that if anything.

"Well, while you had yo' dick up in that hoe, who's been fuckin' everybody in the D, they killed Mylani." The phone line went silent. Deluxe was beyond speechless.

"Did you hear me? Those muthafuckas killed my babies."

Deluxe didn't know whether to be upset about Mylani, or recognize the fact that Rachelle was probably playing him. "What the hell are you talkin' about Unc?"

"Mylani, she's gone, they killed her and our baby!" he screamed.

Deluxe knew that things in Detroit would be crazy after he set things off with Kane and his punk-ass crew, he just never expected for Mylani to get caught in the cross fire. Receiving the news about Mylani, Deluxe would never forget the anguish in his uncle's voice as he told him how brutal her murder was.

With his mind racing a mile a minute all types of thoughts crossed the forefront of his mind. *Mylani was pregnant? Who was behind this? Was it Myth or maybe the Greek? Hell it doesn't matter either way cause there's gonna be hell to pay.* "Listen Unc we'll find out who did this shit, trust me."

"I want this fuckin' city turned outside down."

"I'm on it."

"Leave that bitch's house and do it now!"

Still grief stricken, Gator hung up the phone before Deluxe could get another word out. Deluxe stood in the middle of the floor overcome with anger and sorrow thinking about his plan for revenge. For the first time since he started killing, things became personal for him. The way he figured it, whether or not Myth or Jimmy the Greek was involved, they both had to pay in order for the family to get some satisfaction. On another note, he'd have to deal with the whole Rachelle situation later.

• • • • • • • • • • • • • • • • • • • •

"How in the fuck was I supposed to know that she was pregnant? It's definitely about to be a war in the streets now," Myth suggested, to himself as he thought about the revenge that was sure to come. "I better get my baby mama and son outta here. But first let me find that dumb-ass bitch and her nigga. I gotta get rid of them, which might buy me some time." For the right amount of money, Kandi was sure to rat him out.

Word had quickly spread about Mylani's murder, and

knowing Gator all his life, Myth knew that he wouldn't take this lying down. Plus, Myth was all too familiar with Deluxe's cold style of murder. He remembered how Deluxe had viciously killed Young Bird when he was just a teenager. Not to mention he was now a trained assassin for the Marines. Myth figured that time was not on his side, and if he was going to save his own family he had to make some moves. He needed to throw the scent off of him as quickly as possible. He picked up his phone and quickly called Kandi.

"The streets are real hot because of what you two fuck ups did. To be on the safe side we all need to lay low for a minute. It's only a matter of time before Gator sends some people after you. I got a guy who can get passports so you and that fuckin' dumb-ass man of yours can get out the country. Meet me in the parking garage of the Joe Louis Arena at 3:00 a.m. so we can get this shit straight!" Myth ordered to Kandi, who was now beginning to worry that he was right about Gator finding them.

"We gonna need some more money," she demanded.

Myth wanted to go off, but he had to stay cool. "A'ight just don't be late, we gotta get the fuck outta town."

Myth hung up and grabbed his bullet proof vest, and .45 with the silencer before heading out the door. He figured that the whole passport bit was enough to lure Kandi and her man to the arena where he would lay both of them down for what they'd started. Without there being a big event at the arena, Myth figured that it would be at least daybreak before anyone found their bodies.

Watching from his parked car a few hours later, Myth waited patiently for the arrival of his soon to be marks. As the minutes passed by, he became even more anxious to carry out the execution. Seeing what appeared to be head lights turning into the parking garage, Myth grabbed his gat, hopped out of the car, then ducked real low behind his tire. "Right on time."

When the metallic red BMW was in plain site, Myth shook his head back and forth, especially when he saw Kandi in the driver's seat. "After all the shit that don' went down, her dumb-ass got a nerve to be drivin' Mylani's car. How stupid can that bitch be? Now I know I gotta get rid of they ass," he said to himself.

As the car got even closer, it was the perfect time for Myth to spring from behind his car. Standing up, he squeezed the trigger of his street sweeper causing Kandi to violently lose control and hit a huge concrete column. Not wanting to take the risk of leaving either one of them alive, Myth walked over to the smoking car and unloaded the remaining shells in the clip of his gun into the bodies of Kandi and her partner. As planned, Myth didn't leave behind any witnesses, but what he did make sure to leave was a little surprise that could possibly implicate Jimmy the Greek.

CHAPTER 12

"Jayson, baby let me tell you again how sorry I am about Mylani. I know she was like an aunt to you. How do you think Gator is doing?" Rachelle asked, as she kissed Deluxe's neck. She'd spent the night over Gator's house to help console him.

"With everything that I've had to go through, I would've never thought that something like this would happen to her. And for her to die in such a fucked up way, is just…fucked up. Gator's taking it hard. Mylani didn't even get a chance to tell him that she was pregnant," Deluxe replied, while rubbing his head trying to massage the hurt and anger out. "Damn, first my father and now this."

"I know the entire thing is mind blowing."

"Thank you for being here for me baby girl," Deluxe said, as he pulled Rachelle closer to him.

"Come on, you don't think that I would let you go through this alone do you?" she replied, as her soft juicy lips met his.

"All of this shit got me thinkin' about what's important in life and what's important to me is my family," Deluxe confided to the woman that had held a special part of his heart for many years.

Wrapping her arms around him again, Rachelle told Deluxe that she would be there to help him get through the entire process. No matter what the two of them went through, Deluxe had always been able to count on Rachelle to be there for him when it counted the most. He wanted to tell her thank you and that he needed her, but for some reason he kept thinking about what Gator had mentioned to him the night before. Even though they were not in a serious relationship, the fact that Rachelle could possible be sucking every dick in town still bothered him.

The special moment that they were beginning to share was interrupted when his cell phone rang. After looking at the caller ID, this time Deluxe didn't even think twice about answering. "How you holdin' up, Unc?" a frustrated Deluxe asked, trying to gauge if Gator was better than the night before.

"So, what did you find out?"

"Well, I drove around for a while last night and asked damn near everybody I saw if they'd heard anythin' about the murder, but came up short."

"Oh yeah. Well obviously you didn't ask the right people, 'cause I got some info that we need to check into already," Gator replied.

"Cool, are you comin' back to the house?"

Gator let out a deep sigh. "Naa, I can't come there right now especially knowin' that my baby ain't never comin' back. Meet me at Momma's…" Gator stopped in his tracks once he heard a female's voice in the background. "Who the fuck is that?"

"Oh, it's Rachelle. She came over last night to try and help me get through this."

Gator was beyond furious. "What? Muthafucka, are you crazy? I don't bring no bitches to my house and neither should you. No wonder yo' ass ain't on fuckin' point!"

"Trust me Unc, I'm on point."

"Besides, didn't I fuckin' warn yo' ass last night that she been openin' up her pussy to every nigga in the D? Were you not listenin' to me damnit?"

"Yeah I was but…"

"But what. Look at first I wasn't gonna tell you this shit, but fuck it now. After the way my life is goin' what else do I have to lose. I fucked Rachelle a few months ago, so that bitch ain't really lookin' out for you like you think she is."

Deluxe was speechless and didn't know whether to be mad at Rachelle or his uncle. However, at the moment, both people seemed to be worthy of a bullet to the head.

"This is the reason why I tried to tell you to stay away from her, 'cause the bitch is scandalous. Nephew, ain't no more good girls in the D, just in case you wonderin',"" Gator continued.

"Why didn't you tell me?"

"Cause she begged me not too. I probably would've still kept that shit to myself, but since you been spendin' so much time wit' her ass, I thought you should know. Deluxe I need you to be focused. We don't have time for pussy right now, especially some tainted pussy like Rachelle's. She still got that tattoo of some cherry juice dripping down the crack of her ass?"

Deluxe glanced over at Rachelle with complete disgust. "Thanks for finally warnin' me." He was careful not to answer his uncle's question.

"Now, get that bitch out my house!"

"Bet. I'll be over Momma Ruth's in a few."

When Deluxe got off the phone, he didn't waste anytime gathering Rachelle's belongings. He grabbed her purse along with a pair of crystal studded flip flops, and stuffed them into her overnight bag. She looked at him with confusion.

"What are you doing?"

"Gettin' yo' shit so you can get the fuck out my uncle's house."

Rachelle was still confused. "Why? I thought you wanted me here?"

"Yeah well, I thought I was the only one is this family who

you was fuckin', but I guess I was wrong."

The look on Rachelle's face instantly said that she was *guilty*. As if she was scared to death, Rachelle took a deep breath, exhaled, and then closed her eyes.

"Didn't yo' stupid-ass know that I would eventually find out about it? Of all people why him?" Deluxe asked, obviously hurt at the thought of Gator having his way with the woman he once loved. "Damn, is every bitch in his city on money?"

The viciousness in Deluxe's tone took Rachelle by surprise, leaving her speechless. Tears began to well up in her eyes as Deluxe looked at her with pure hatred in his heart. She was terrified of what he might do.

Still overwhelmed with emotion, all she could muster in between sniffles was, "I'm so sorry Jayson. It was a huge mistake. I was so drunk that night and Gator took advantage of me."

Deluxe stopped walking around the room and looked at her. "You know a wise man once said, you may make mistakes, but you a failure when you start blaming someone else." He continued to stare at Rachelle who was balling by this point. "So, were you drunk when you fucked all those other niggas? Word on the street is that you a hoe."

Puzzled at his response, she could only ask "What are you talking about. I haven't been fucking other dudes. Just you."

"Yeah right, and you expect me to believe that shit. As a matter of fact, I need you to go." With most of her stuff in his hand, Deluxe walked to the front door, and then threw every single item outside.

"Why are you doing this?" Rachelle pleaded.

"Because I'm dealin' wit' a lying bitch, that's why. Now, I'm not gonna tell you again to get the fuck out. The next time, I'll put you out myself."

Seeing that Deluxe was serious, Rachelle slowly walked toward the door, wearing a pair of sheer purple pajamas. Her plan was to turn around and plead with Deluxe one last time, but as soon as she made it outside, he slammed the door so hard it almost came off the hinges.

● ●

During the drive over to his grandmother's house on Ardmore Street, Deluxe had a million thoughts running through his head. He couldn't help but think about how Rachelle didn't deny that she and Gator had slept together. Of all the people that she could've fucked, Deluxe wondered why she'd stooped so low. He wondered if it was for the money, or was his uncle really trying to take everything that he loved and make it his own. Thoughts of Gator fucking Rachelle sent Deluxe into a rage on the inside as he continued to drive down the highway to meet the very man that he was for some reason beginning to hate.

However, despite having those feelings toward his uncle for what he'd done, Deluxe knew that he had to put his game face on. Besides, he still felt loyal to the man who'd raised him. After all, it was the same man who'd taught Deluxe that women couldn't be trusted and to never put money or loyalty over a bitch. Deluxe knew that he had to put his thoughts of disgust aside and be there for the family and find out who was behind Mylani's murder.

"I definitely plan on revisitin' this shit again," Deluxe mentioned to himself as he pressed on the gas.

Pulling up to his grandmother's house he sat out front for a minute trying to pull himself together and get his mind right. He knew that from here on out, he was going to have to be on top of his game. Niggas had stepped over boundaries. No one was safe; not him, Gator, or Momma Ruth. "Shit, them muthafuckas ain't safe either," he said, to himself as he finally exited the rental car.

Greeted at the door by Momma Ruth, she reached out her hands to hug her grieving grandson. "Hey baby, how are you?"

"I'm holdin' on. How are you?"

"I'm hurt but trying to stay strong for my son."

Not only was Deluxe worried about Gator, but his grandmother as well. She and Mylani had grown a bond over the years and were just like mother and daughter. Mylani had lost her own mother to breast cancer when she graduated from college, so when she and Gator got together his grandmother was immediately drawn to her. Momma Ruth thought that she was the most decent girl that his uncle had ever brought home, and always treated her as such.

"Wow, he's in pretty bad shape huh?" Deluxe asked, as he walked into the house and toward the basement where he was sure Gator could be found.

"Yeah he's down there," Momma Ruth replied. "Jayson, please look after your uncle. You got more sense than he does, and I don't want him to do nothing stupid. I can't handle losing another child. I done lost your father and now that sweet girl and my un-born grandbaby. I don't wanna lose Gerald too. You hear me?" Momma Ruth questioned as Deluxe looked at the anguish in her eyes.

"Don't worry Granny. I'ma take care of everythin'," he answered, before disappearing into the grim lit basement. Little did his grandmother know just how much Deluxe was planning on handling the situation.

As he walked down the steps, Deluxe could smell the burning fragrance of a French vanilla incense while Al Green's old classic, '*For the Good Times*' played in the background. Seeing his nephew come around the corner, Gator took another swig from his glass of Cognac with his left hand while he held on to the 9mm that was firmly planted in his right.

"I ain't never loved another woman like her Nephew," his uncle confessed, while wiping the tears from his face.

"Any word on who did this shit?" the young seething killer asked, while pouring himself a shot of the Cognac.

"Hell yeah. Word on the street is police found that stripper bitch Kandi and a nigga dead in Mylani's car this mornin' so more than likely them muthafuckas had somethin' to do wit' it."

Deluxe was completely shocked. After seeing Kandi at Belle Isle that night, he knew she was on money hard, but he never thought she would do something like this. "So, who do you think put Kandi up to it 'cause I know her dumb-ass didn't think of that shit herself?" Deluxe inquired after taking a sip of his drink.

"I'm not sure, but whoever it was they want me to think Jimmy did it cause word done got back that a Mr. Alan's Shoe bag full of money was found inside the car too." Gator let out a huge sigh. "Actually Nephew anybody could've pulled this shit off. Jimmy, Myth, and a whole lot of hatin' ass niggas in the street who want me to go away. Because of that, every fuckin' body gotta die," Gator instructed.

If it was Jimmy he probably woulda been bolder about that shit, so it's gotta be Myth, Deluxe thought to himself.

CHAPTER 13

Deluxe pulled into the parking lot of the Swanson Funeral Home on East Grand Blvd. three days later looking for anything or anyone that might seem a little out of place or the least bit suspicious. He figured that today of all days, Gator would be the most vulnerable to a set up. Mylani's funeral was the biggest news of the city, and up until now, no one was able to hit Gator where it would hurt the most.

After seeing that the parking lot was clear, Deluxe ensured that his Glock was tucked away securely on his side. He hoped that today of all days he wouldn't have to let his trusted friend sing to anyone, but with the streets being the way they were, he wasn't going to take any chances. Looking around one last time, he decided to go inside the funeral home and spend a few minutes alone with Mylani before the service. A service that would not include any singing or a trip to the cemetery. Gator had made it very clear that he didn't want to see his girl put in the ground, so that part was scheduled to be done privately.

When Deluxe walked inside the cool building, the owner,

Mr. Baker, took him to the room where the service was going to be held. This was the first time that Deluxe had stepped inside of a funeral home since his father was murdered. He didn't like the coldness, the quietness, or the stench of death that filled the air and clogged his nose.

Deluxe walked down the isle that led to the high quality $4000.00 solid mahogany casket that Momma Ruth hand picked. Even though Gator was unable to participate in any of the funeral arrangements, he made sure that Momma Ruth chose the best accommodations for his girl. As Deluxe drew closer to the casket, he looked at the numerous flower bouquets and thought about how Mylani didn't deserve the vicious and monstrous death she'd endured, and all because of who her fiancé was. Finally standing next to the casket, Deluxe bent down and kissed her on the forehead. Despite her lifeless features, Mylani was still beautiful, especially in her favorite cream silk Marc Jacobs dress. Touching her cold stiff hand, he eyed the beautiful engagement ring that his uncle had given to her years ago and quietly began to sob. Deluxe told her how sorry he was that she had to pay for the sins of his uncle, and that he would do whatever it took to make everyone pay who was involved with her murder.

As Deluxe tried to get himself together before the crowd came, he remembered that his uncle had taught him that crying was for the weak, and that real g's didn't shed tears, especially in the public eye. Deluxe pulled a handkerchief out of his suit pocket and wiped away the tears that were freely falling down his stressed face. The funeral was scheduled to start soon and now more than ever he needed to be on his 'A' game. With Gator being one of the cities most feared and notorious gangsters there was the ever-present possibility that Mylani's funeral would bring out not only the cities elite, but the wanna-be killers as well. Deluxe couldn't allow his grief to cause him to lose focus.

Fifteen minutes later, Deluxe heard the mumblings of a few people walking into the room. When he turned around to see who it was, he saw Momma Ruth, Gator, and a foot soldier that his uncle had obviously brought along with him. Deluxe knew that the man was packing heat from the long trench coat he wore, especially by it being July. It was a dead giveaway.

"Go post up in the back," Gator ordered to the soldier. "I don't think nobody is crazy enough to come through the front."

Immediately, the soldier did as he was told. Even though Gator had Deluxe he needed the extra man power to stand guard just in case anything popped off, it was Deluxe's responsibility to focus on protecting Gator and Momma Ruth if anything went south.

Carrying two-dozen long stemmed red and white roses,

Gator escorted Momma Ruth down the aisle with his head slightly lowered. Looking like she was an usher at a local church, Momma Ruth wore an all white dress with a big white and pink hat. She refused to wear dark colors at a funeral. Like the gangster he was, Gator was decked out in a black Armani three-button suit, along with a pair of his handcrafted alligator shoes, and a Humphrey Bogart looking fedora hat. The dark Prada shades that adorned his eyes disguised the hurt, guilt and anguish that he was feeling as he knew that this would be the last time he ever saw his one true love.

Deluxe gave Gator the traditional what's up head nod, as he walked toward his grieving uncle and grandmother to show them his support.

"I'll take Momma Ruth to her seat Unc," Deluxe suggested, while extending his hand. "Go ahead and spend some time wit' Mylani."

Without verbally responding, Gator just nodded and slowly strolled over to the casket where his once beautiful queen laid. For the first time since he'd become a hustler, Gator was starting to feel like none of the cars, jewelry, fame or money was worth the price that was being paid to have it all. He stood next to the casket shaking his head as tears rolled down his crater filled face in waterfall fashion.

Laying the flowers on top of the casket, Gator knelt down

next to it. With his head hung down in a defeated state he whim-
pered, "I'm so sorry baby, I'm so sorry. I never meant for anything
to happen to you. I swear on my unborn seed, I'ma make whoever
did this to you pay."

Seeing how distraught her son was, Momma Ruth asked
Deluxe to go and get Gator and help him to his seat next to her on
the front row. Deluxe agreed and walked over to his ailing uncle.

"Come on Unc. People are about to come in and Momma
Ruth needs you right now," Deluxe whispered.

Looking at his nephew through the dark shades, Gator
shook his head and weakly walked with Deluxe toward the chairs
where his mother quietly sat. Stopping before they reached
Momma Ruth, Gator finally broke his silence as his whispered to
Deluxe. "They took my heart from me Nephew. Those muthafuckas killed my babies. I don't want a soul left breathin' when this
shit is all over wit'." Removing his shades to emphasize his point,
Gator repeated, "Not a fuckin' soul left'," before sitting down.

"We gon' get 'em Unc, that's my word." Deluxe replied as
he took a seat next to his uncle.

• •

In typical Detroit fashion, the scene at the funeral was more
like a Players Ball than a memorial service. The majority of
Gator's criminal affiliates showed up in supreme fashion. Every

kind of car from Bentley Phantom's and Porsche's to Mercedes and Jags they were all lined up outside the funeral home. Hustla's from all over the state were coming to pay their respects to their comrades' fallen queen. Fatboy from Flint, Big Kat and Toot from Pontiac, and Gutta from Saginaw, his closest allies outside of Detroit, all strolled up the isle toward Gator. Even the young cat, Premo who Gator didn't care for at all showed up.

Gator was happy that his cohorts had gone out of their way to show him and his family some love. He sat and watched as more and more people walked up to the casket to view the remains of his better half. One by one, they all stopped in front of him to shake his hand and offer their condolences or words of encouragement, which Gator truly appreciated. There were a lot of familiar faces coming to show their deepest sympathy, however as one familiar face approached him, Gator's eyes grew three sizes almost sending him into a frenzy.

"Look, I know you think I probably had somethin' to do wit' this shit, but you wrong. I was wit' my baby mother the night Mylani was killed," the familiar voice said.

"You got some muthafuckin' nerve to bring yo' bitch-ass around here after what you probably did?" Gator yelled as he stared violently at his former friend. "I should kill yo' ass right now muthafucka!" he spat, as Myth gritted his teeth.

"Yeah nigga where the fuck you been hidin'?" Deluxe chimed in. "I been lookin' for yo' ass."

Momma Ruth was furious. "Jayson, stop that cursing right now," she stated in a low tone. "You too Gerald. Pay some respect."

"Look, I done …"

Cutting Myth off in mid sentence, Gator continued ignoring his mother's request. "You don' fucked up is what you should be sayin' nigga! Now get the fuck out before you be the one in the fuckin' casket bitch!"

Myth looked around at all the people sitting in the room, who stared at him like they were watching a movie on the big screen. All that was missing was the bag of butter popcorn. He wasn't about to lose his respect in front of all those people. "A'ight fuck it then!" Myth yelled as he stormed out of the funeral home.

"Gerald Green, what is wrong with you? Have you lost your mind? I didn't raise you to act like this, especially at a funeral," Momma Ruth scolded as the crowded room looked on in shock.

Still ignoring his mother, Gator turned to Deluxe. "I can't believe he had the balls to show his face around here like shit is sweet. Don't he know I'ma find out if he really had somethin' to do wit' this shit?" he whispered, so Momma Ruth couldn't hear. "I want that muthafucka in a body bag."

Deluxe shook his head. "Don't worry. It's a done deal."

Minutes later, after all of the commotion between Gator and Myth had calmed down, the MC of the hour, Reverend Atkins took his place behind the maple wood podium. The funeral home was standing room only as the Reverend adjusted the microphone.

"Let us all bow our heads in prayer," Reverend Atkins commanded in a sincere tone as he stared at the large crowd.

Everyone in the room bowed their head. After a stirring prayer, the small minister who had a slight overbite was about to begin the eulogy when the service was once again interrupted by loud whispers from the crowd. Turning around to see what was going on, Gator was fumed with rage when he saw, Sonny and Jimmy the Greek walking up the isle toward Mylani's open casket.

"What the fuck are y'all doin' here?" Gator boasted. He could care less what Momma Ruth thought of his behavior now.

Taking immediate action, Deluxe grabbed Gator's arm. "Unc, sit tight. This ain't the time or place."

"The young boy is right Gator, sit tight," the fat Greek man replied with smirk on his face. "This is not the time or the place for whatever you might be thinking."

"Okay maybe you didn't hear me the first time. What the fuck are you doin' here Jimmy?" Gator repeated. Now standing face to face with his enemy.

"Lord have mercy," Momma Ruth belted out while holding her chest. She looked at Reverend Atkins, who'd grabbed his bible and stepped back a few inches.

"Now is that any way to talk to an old friend Gator?" the slimy man asked, in a condescending tone. "I came to pay my respects to such a beautiful woman." With a smirk on his face, Jimmy looked over at the casket. "It's too bad you had to be the one to pay the price."

Flying into a rage, Gator shouted, "Did you have somethin' to do wit' this muthafucka?"

"Maybe, maybe not. Just know this, you fuckin' nigger, nobody disrespects me and doesn't pay a price for it," Jimmy remarked, with a sly grin on his face.

The entire crowd started mumbling amongst themselves.

Laughing in Gator's face, Jimmy turned to Sonny. "You see this why it doesn't pay to do business with niggers. Rock or Myth would've never pulled a stunt like this. Shit, it looks like Myth might be the real brains behind this operation away. "

At the mention of his brother's name, and crediting Myth for the success of his business, Gator snapped and pulled out his 9mm before lunging toward Jimmy at full speed. Immediately, Sonny pulled out his chrome Smith & Wesson .38 causing Deluxe to grab his gun as well. Seeing that the once peaceful occasion had turned into an all out war zone, everyone started screaming and running toward the door.

"Jesus!" Momma Ruth screamed.

Reverend Atkins bowed his head and immediately started praying.

"So what's it gonna be? Put the gun away or I'm killin' yo' fuckin' boss," Deluxe demanded, as he stared violently at Sonny.

However, before Sonny or Jimmy could say anything, the foot soldier that was guarding the back door ran into the room with his AK-47 drawn after hearing all the commotion. Seeing that they were out numbered and sure to die if he made one wrong move, Sonny slowly began to lower his gun.

Jimmy looked at Momma Ruth, whose tears clouded her vision. With her arms folded, she rocked back and forth at a fast pace. "It looks like you've upset the old lady," he stated in his thick Greek accent. Both Gator and Deluxe quickly looked at Momma Ruth, but directed their attention right back to Sonny, the man with the gun. "You're in deep shit now my friend. The money that you used to owe me is the least of your worries," Jimmy said, with an evil smile that stretched across his decaying face.

"What the fuck are you talkin' 'bout?" Gator asked.

"Let's just say, I got all my money back with interest,"

Jimmy continued before he and his flunky slowly began to make their way toward the exit.

"You fat muthafucka, what the hell do you mean you got all of your money back wit' interest?" Gator asked waving his gun. "You know what, fuck both of you greek muthafuckas."

However, before Jimmy could reply, Sonny raised his .38 back again. "No, fuck you mooley nigger!"

Within seconds, complete chaos erupted. Gator, Deluxe and Sonny all started shooting at each other as the few remaining people in the crowded room began to scatter like roaches. In the midst of all of the commotion, the soldier who Gator had brought with him caught a slug to the middle of his forehead, splattering his brains all over a lady that was trying to hide underneath a chair.

As Gator ran toward Sonny and Jimmy who were trying to escape out the front door, he yelled to Deluxe, "Get Momma the fuck outta here!"

Since she was no longer in sight, Deluxe quickly wondered where Momma Ruth was hiding. Running toward the first row of chairs, he said a silent prayer hoping that she'd found a safe place. Unfortunately, it didn't take long to realize his prayers would never be answered. Looking at the carnage that was left in the wake of the shootout, Deluxe was not prepared for what he saw.

"Noooo...Oh God please.... No!" Deluxe screamed, as he

approached his grandmother's lifeless body. "Nooo….Momma

Ruth get up!" he cried, in an agonizing voice. But the only reaction

Deluxe saw was the oozing blood from her temple.

CHAPTER 14

Deluxe ignored all the commotion inside of the funeral home as he continued to hold Momma Ruth's frail body. The celebration of life had turned into a bloody massacre, leaving Momma Ruth, the foot soldier and even Reverend Atkins all dead. Still in a state of shock, Deluxe didn't hear Gator calling his name.

"Deluxe…Deluxe, we gotta get the fuck up outta here before the cops come!"

Gator was screaming as he headed toward Deluxe who was rocking back and forth with Momma Ruth in his arms.

"I was supposed to protect her," Deluxe sobbed.

"Look muthafucka we gotta go. She's dead and ain't shit we can do 'bout that now. Put her the fuck down and come on!"

Deluxe couldn't believe that Gator was telling him to leave his own mother's dead body on the floor as if she was a dog they'd found on the side of the road. Overcome with anger and grief, Deluxe looked at his uncle and yelled, "Someone put a bullet through yo' fuckin' mother's head and you tellin' me to just leave her here. What the fuck is wrong wit' you?"

"Look nigga we at a fuckin' funeral home. These mutha-fucka's can take care of this shit for us. We gotta get outta!" Gator yelled at Deluxe coldly.

Realizing that neither one of them needed to be there when the police arrived, Deluxe nodded his head in agreement. Kissing Momma Ruth on the forehead as he gently held her, he whispered, "Granny, I swear on everythin', I'm gonna make those mutha-fuckas pay for doin' this to you." He kissed her on the cheek and continued to rock back and forth with her cold limp body cradled in his arms. Deluxe looked up and saw Gator yelling at the funeral director and pointing in the direction of Momma Ruth.

"Look the cops will be here in a fuckin' minute." He reached in his pocket and pulled out a small stack of money. "Here take this money and do whatever the fuck you need to do to take care of my mother." Gator stuffed the cash into the trembling di-rector's pocket. "If you need more, then I'll get it to you."

"I…I can't take…this money. I don't want any parts to…this mess," Mr. Baker stuttered. "You need to wait for the cops."

Gator clenched his jaw before pulling out his gun and quickly stuffing it in Mr. Baker's mouth. "Muthafucka are you tryin' to be funny?"

Mr. Baker shook his head as fear consumed his facial expression.

"I see that I need to remind you of some important details," Gator taunted. "Remember, when the cops get here and start askin' questions, you didn't see shit. And most importantly, you don't know shit. You got that?"

Mr. Baker quickly shook his head.

"Good, 'cause I would hate to come back, and put you in one of them fuckin' caskets you sell." After removing the gun from Mr. Baker's mouth, and scaring the funeral director half to death, Gator turned to Deluxe. "Let's go!"

Seeing that Deluxe was still shaken, Gator ran over to where his nephew was and pulled him away from his mother. Letting her body fall to the ground, Deluxe reluctantly got up as tears stained his face. Setting his sights on his uncle, Deluxe hissed, "You worried about Mr. Baker, what about everybody else who was here?"

"I ain't worried about them muthafucka's either. They know the deal. Now stop actin' like a bitch, and let's go."

Within seconds, Gator and Deluxe quickly made their way out the doors of the funeral home, making their escape from the blood bath, before the police swarmed the building looking for answers. They jumped into Gator's car, and sped out of the parking lot like professional stunt drivers. Still pissed with his uncle for leaving Momma Ruth like that, Deluxe looked at Gator with disgust.

"So what the fuck are we gonna do now?"

"Look, I know you ready to go bust a cap in somebody. Trust me we'll get them fools back for what they did to Momma. But we really need to find out what the fuck Jimmy meant when he said somethin' 'bout gettin' his money back wit' interest."

"Are you serious? Why are we doin' this shit now? All you care about is money. If anythin' we need to be goin' somewhere to lay low for awhile."

Gator looked at Deluxe without any emotion. "Shit, that's only gon' make the cops even more suspicious. And why the fuck are you askin' me so many questions anyway? Besides, you better take that fuckin' base out yo' voice, and think about more important things like gettin' yo' muthafuckin' mind right. If I find out some foul shit 'bout my money, it's really gon' be time for war nigga!"

"So, Momma Ruth wasn't important?"

"Deluxe you really fuckin' testin' me right now."

Glaring out the window, as Gator picked up speed, Deluxe whispered, "What the fuck ever man, I'm tired of this shit!"

In the past, Deluxe was always prepared to prove his loyalty and do whatever it took for his uncle and the family. But now things had taken a drastic turn for the worst. Besides his father, he'd lost the two most innocent and important people in his life, so being a pawn in his uncle's web of deceit wasn't worth it anymore.

I gotta get the fuck outta this game before it kills me, Deluxe thought to himself as he continued to sit, gazing out the window.

Within a few minutes they pulled up across the street from Gator's other dope house on the east side of town. Putting the car in park, Gator turned off the engine before looking at Deluxe. "Let's go in here and see if everythin' is on point, Nephew."

Still in disbelief about how nonchalant his uncle was about Momma Ruth being murdered, Deluxe replied solemnly, "I'm not going."

Gator put his hand up to his ear like he was hard of hearing. "What the fuck did you just say?"

"I said I'm not going. If you more concerned about money then yo' own mother then do this shit by yo'self."

While listening to his nephew's new opinion about the situation, Gator became furious. "So you gonna bitch up on me again and act like one of these pussy-ass niggas out here in the street?" Fuming at Deluxe's blatant disrespect Gator continued to tear into him, "I raised you to have more heart than this, and now you wanna act all soft and shit."

"What the fuck did you just say to me muthafucka?" Deluxe replied, as he stared at his uncle with death in his eyes. "Was I soft when I killed Detective Hughes for yo' bitch ass? When you were too muthafuckin' scared to do it yourself," he added.

"Watch what the fuck you say Nephew. You don't wanna bite the hand that feeds you!"

"I don't give a shit about yo' threats anymore."

Gator began to bang the steering wheel with his fist. "Nigga, if it wasn't for me where would yo' lame-ass be, huh? I raised you. I can't believe you sittin' here disrespectin' me like this!" Gator yelled.

"If it wasn't for you, Mylani and Momma Ruth would still be alive," Deluxe shot back. "I don't know who the fuck you think you are, but don't forget yo' punk-ass wouldn't be nothin' without me. You get the respect out here in these streets because of the work that I put in. You over here barkin' about some bullshit ass money, and Momma Ruth is cross town with her muthafuckin' head split open. Fuck this I'm out!"

As Deluxe opened the car door, and proceeded to get out, Gator pulled on his arm. He was beyond furious, but knew he had to remain calm. In reality, the only person left in his corner was Deluxe, so making the situation any worse would be detrimental to his whole operation. He couldn't allow that to happen.

"Look Nephew, I'm just as upset as you are 'bout what happened to Momma, but let's be honest, you know she loved Rock way more than she loved me. So, I guess I always resented her for that shit," Gator admitted.

Deluxe took a deep breath and shook his head from side to side. "Well, maybe so, but you still don't have to act like she ain't even fuckin' dead."

"I know she dead, but I still gotta get my paper."

Thinking about what Gator said, Deluxe shook his head in disgust. "I'm tired of this shit. I've had enough." Without waiting for a reply, Deluxe got out the car and slammed the door, then stormed toward the opposite direction of the dope house.

Running behind any dude in broad daylight was not an option for Gator.

"Well, if that's how you wanna roll fine, but you know the rules to this game. The only way you leavin' out this fam is in a muthafuckin' body bag," Gator spoke out loud.

CHAPTER 15

Days passed, and several homicide detectives investigating Momma Ruth's murder had stopped by Gator's house and drywall business to ask him what he knew about the murder. In typical gangster fashion, Gator told the detectives that he didn't know shit, and if they would get on their job instead of harassing him, they might find the killer. His reluctance to cooperate made the detectives even more suspicious of him, so they knew Gator was holding something back. However, with no evidence, and no witnesses willing to come forward, the case was cold for the moment.

With the police sweating him, and his relationship with the last loyal person on the team crumbling right before his eyes, Gator's stress mounted. Things were so bad between him and Deluxe that during the private viewing of Momma Ruth's body before she was laid to rest, they paid their last respects at separate times. To make matters worse, Gator's second dope house had indeed been robbed. Now, with all his coke and large sums of money gone, Myth and Jimmy still lurking on the streets, and the desperate need for another connect, Gator knew he had to make things right with Deluxe as soon as possible.

Gator sat behind the desk of his home office with a glass of Hennessy and a few lines of white horse that he was beginning to snort more frequently. He replayed the events of Mylani's funeral and what Jimmy said over and over in his head.

"I know that fat muthafucka was the one who took my money and the rest of my shit. That's the fuckin' interest he was talkin' 'bout," Gator said to himself as he snorted the remaining lines of coke then tilted his head back.

"I gotta get the fuck back on. I need to call Deluxe and iron this shit out, so we can move on to business. Hopefully he's not still actin' like a bitch."

Gator also needed to talk to Deluxe and come up with a game plan to get at Jimmy before he tried to get at him first. Wanting to go ahead and get a plan set in motion, Gator wiped some coke from the tip of his nose, then flipped open his cell phone to call his nephew.

"Yeah?" Deluxe answered after several rings. He didn't seem too enthused.

"What up Nephew? How you been holdin' up?"

Hesitant to answer, Deluxe replied, "I'm good, just been thinkin' about all the shit that's goin' on. Why, what's up?"

Gator let out a huge sigh. "Well, I need to talk to you about somethin'. Can you meet me at the MotorCity Casino? I'ma be at my usual spot."

Thinking about whether or not he should meet Gator, Deluxe was quiet for a moment before replying. "A'ight gimmie about thirty minutes. I'll be there."

Without giving a reply, Gator closed his phone and thought for minute about what he was going to say to Deluxe in order to get him back on the team.

● ●

On the way to the casino, Deluxe thought about how he should just leave town and be done with his uncle for good, instead of dealing with him again. However, after overextending his leave, Deluxe knew that if he went back to North Carolina the Marine Corps would charge him with being AWOL and throw his ass in jail. Even a few of his fellow soldiers had been calling him over the past few days. More than likely they were trying to see what had happened to him, but Deluxe didn't answer. At this point he was beginning to feel that jail was the best place for him. At least in jail, he wouldn't have to worry about killing anyone else and more importantly anyone killing him.

Just like clockwork, it took Deluxe thirty minutes to arrive at the MotorCity Casino, which was situated in the heart of downtown Detroit. Pulling up to the luxury hotel, Deluxe left his faithful rental car with the valet and made his way toward the lobby. As soon as he stepped inside, the loud sounds of slot machines almost drowned his hearing. On his way to the Overdrive Lounge, Deluxe figured that Gator wanted to talk to him about finding Myth or getting rid of Jimmy. But at this stage in the game he just wanted to cut ties and count his losses.

However, deep down he knew that any plans of retiring would only cause more problems between him and the only father figure he'd ever known. Gator had always preached loyalty to Deluxe, and by not wanting to continue in the killing game that would be the ultimate sign of disloyalty in Gator's eyes. Deluxe knew in his heart that the only way out of this life was jail or the grave, either his or Gator's.

Snapping out of his trance as he entered the lounge, Deluxe saw Gator seated at his usual spot, a round table tucked away in the corner. He was sitting on the leather sectional wearing a button down Ferragamo shirt, a pair of slacks and drinking a glass of what appeared to be Hennessey and Coke. The tension was thick as Deluxe approached the table; the two once strong allies stared at each other like bitter enemies.

"What up Gator?" Deluxe asked while getting comfortable at the table.

"Oh, so I'm Gator now? What, we not family no more?"

Deluxe looked at his uncle, who appeared to be high. "You a'ight?"

"Yeah I'm a'ight nigga. Shit, don't I look a'ight. I'm dressed to muthafuckin' impress," Gator answered, while whipping the clear mucus coming from his nose. "What you drinkin'?"

Deluxe stared at him for a second. "Uhh...just water."

"Water? Damn boy you just like yo' pops! That nigga always wanted water or a damn soda or somethin' when we were out. Shit, you even look like that nigga today," Gator said, wiping his nose again. His strange behavior had definitely caught Deluxe's attention.

"I'm just tryin' to stay focused," Deluxe replied. *Shit, like yo' ass should be.*

In reality, Gator hated how much Deluxe reminded him of his brother. He hated their laid back demeanors, their confidence, charm, and even worse he hated their nonchalant attitude at times. All of the things that Gator deemed to be a weakness in Rock, he saw the same weakness in Deluxe. Gator even hated the fact that Rock had a son and he didn't.

Deluxe knew as well that he reminded Gator of his father. He'd been told all of his life, how much he looked like Rock, and as he got older how much he acted like him too. However, this was the first time he really knew how much it bothered his uncle.

"You know I miss that nigga Rock, right?" Gator asked.

I wish he would stop talkin' about this shit. Why the fuck is he actin' so crazy? "Yeah I know what you mean. Not a day goes by that I don't think about my pops. I really wanna know who came at him and why."

Shrugging off his nephew's persistence in knowing who killed his father, Gator spoke up. "You know me and him came up in this game together. Me, him and Myth. But Rock was just, I'on know, different from us. He was really laid back and almost passive to a fault. I mean don't get me wrong, that nigga knew how to handle his business, but it was like he didn't have that same killer instinct that I had, and niggas thought that he was weak for that. I guess that's why they came at him instead of me. He got caught slippin' out here and it cost him his life."

Laughing to himself, Gator reached into his pocket and pulled out a fresh Cuban cigar and ran it under his nose to smell the freshness of the tightly rolled tobacco. Barely taking his eyes off Deluxe, Gator pulled out his platinum and diamond encrusted cigar cutter from his pocket, cut the end, then stuck it in his mouth. After lighting the cigar, Gator took a couple of puffs and blew rings of smoke in Deluxe's direction.

Unfazed by his uncle's disrespectful attempts to get him to break his cool, Deluxe thought to himself, *something is definitely wrong wit' this nigga. Shit I guess I need to start keepin' an eye out for his ass too.*

"Any luck findin' Myth's faggot-ass yet?"

Deluxe shook his head. "I haven't been lookin'."

Gator was upset, but didn't want to show how pissed he was about Deluxe not being focused and basically not giving a shit. "Listen, I need you to be on yo' fuckin' 'A' game. We still got a lot of work to do out here. I got us a couple of tickets to Cabo to meet wit' Chico. We gotta get a new connect fast."

Gator slid the ticket across the table to Deluxe, who looked at the paper with the least bit of emotion. Shaking his head in disapproval, Deluxe slid the ticket back over.

"Nah I'm good. You go handle yo' business."

Boiling over with anger by this point, Gator began to shake his legs uncontrollably in order to try and calm himself down. He needed to come up with plan fast. "Look Nephew, how 'bout this. I'll challenge you to a poker match. If I win, you better be on that plane to Mexico. But if I lose, which I'm sure I won't, you don't have to go."

"Man, is this why you called me?"

Gator placed the ticket back in his pocket. "Do you think I wanna be sittin' here bettin' a nigga to go wit' me somewhere? I ain't never had to do no shit like this."

Looking at his uncle, who now seemed to be getting high off his own supply, Deluxe contemplated the bet in his head for a few minutes before finally deciding to accept.

Staring at each other coldly in the eyes as they stood up, the duo headed over to the High Limit Gaming Room for a game of No Limit Texas Hold'em. As they approached the room they were greeted by a huge six foot nine inch security guard, whose job was to keep people out who didn't have the $1000.00 minimum bet or the clout to be in the room. Gator possessed both, the money and the clout, and everyone in the room knew it. He was a regular in the High Limit Gaming area.

It was actually in the same room that he and Rock first met Jimmy the Greek. Even though Rock didn't gamble, he watched on as the two battled each other for more than three hours in a game of high stakes winner take all seven card stud, with Gator walking away with seventy-five thousand dollars of Jimmy's money. Impressed by Gator's winnings and the fact that he had enough money to cover the bets, Jimmy invited Gator and Rock to one of his clubs so that the two could get better acquainted and discuss possibly doing business with each other.

"Welcome back Mr. Green, will you be having your usual table?" the pit boss asked, as Gator and Deluxe walked through the entrance.

"Yeah Bill, you know how I get down," Gator responded, poking out his chest in confidence.

"Right this way gentleman. Amanda will be your dealer this evening. Can I have one of the ladies bring you gentlemen anything to drink?"

"Yeah, tell her bring a bottle of Veuve Clicquot Champagne over. Thank you," Gator instructed. "I'm gonna be celebrating soon."

"Very well sir, enjoy your game."

Looking at the two combatants, the beautiful dealer with dimples said, "Okay gentlemen the game is No Limit Texas Hold'em."

Before Amanda could finish stating the usual terms of the match Gator interrupted her to let her know that tonight's match would be for something worth more than money and that there would only be one hand played. Intrigued by what was about to take place, Amanda looked at her pit boss to gain approval for such a match, which he gladly did. After taking Gator and Deluxe's money, she handed them several black chips. She then shuffled the cards for a few moments and knocked twice on the table to signal to the players and the cameras above that she was about to deal the first card.

With a serious look on his face Gator stared at Deluxe.

Deluxe glared back at his uncle with the look of a trained assassin that was ready to end the life of his next mark. The tension was escalating in the room as the two continued to get into a serious zone, and it didn't take long for a small crowd to emerge. Little did they know, the stakes for Gator this time was higher than any amount of money he's ever bet before. He desperately needed Deluxe to take this trip to Cabo with him to meet with Chico. Without having a new connect, no dope on the streets, and only the money in his pocket left to his name Gator's world was quickly crumbling beneath him.

Snapping out of his trance, Gator took a quick glance at the nine and ten of spades, the dealer passed to him. Thinking that this was his lucky night, Gator decided to up the stakes.

Reaching into his pocket, Gator pulled out a stack of hundred dollar bills. "Let's make this interesting Nephew, here's three grand, let's add this to the bet."

Looking at the two cards that the dealer dealt, Deluxe thought for a moment before replying, "Fuck it I'm in." He tossed thirty one hundred dollar bills in the middle of the table.

Again, the dealer looked at the pit boss for approval before handing the two men even more chips. After finally closing out the bets, Amanda spread three cards out on the table and turned them over revealing a jack of spades, an eight of hearts, and a six of spades. Seeing the cards in front of him, Gator's palms became clammy and wet from the excitement of possibly winning the game. Still showing no emotion, Deluxe took a sneak peek at his cards as he sat back in his chair to wait on the dealers' next move. Sliding a card to the side and knocking on the table again, Amanda turned over a card that was of no help to either of them. Thinking that he was on the verge of victory, Gator pulled out one of his Cuban cigars and rolled it under his nose to take in the savory smell of the illegal tobacco.

"Here's the river card gentleman," Amanda spoke, as she turned over the card that would prove to be the dagger in Gator's heart.

Smiling from ear to ear, Deluxe said, "Damn that has to suck for you Unc. Looks like that six of hearts is the one that just fucked you up huh?" He revealed his six of clubs and five of hearts.

Gator shook his head from side to side with a look of hurt and frustration planted across his crater filled face. "Trips, a fuckin' set of trips beat me," Gator mumbled, as he took a gulp of the champagne. He didn't have the money to lose.

Realizing that he'd just lost one of the most important bets of his life, and his only shot at getting back on his feet, Gator turned to Deluxe who collected his earnings from Amanda, to ask him for a favor. A favor in which he never thought he would have to ask.

"Listen, I know a deals a deal and we made an agreement, but I really need you to take this trip to see Chico wit' me."

Deluxe appeared to be the least bit interested. "Look, right now is not a good time for me. I got a lot of shit I need to work out in my head," Deluxe told his uncle, who was now looking at him with blood shot eyes.

Not wanting to show his complete and utter disgust for Deluxe's lack of loyalty, Gator gritted his teeth. "Well, I need to get some money up and fast. Can you at least dig into the money I know you been stackin' and give me a small loan? I'm kinda low on cash. You heard about the second stash house gettin' hit right?"

Deluxe was caught off guard by his uncle's desperation. In all the years, he'd never seen him like this. Feeling sorry for him, Deluxe just shook his head and laughed. "Maybe you shouldn't make bets you can't win. Ain't that what you always told me?"

"Muthafucka, if it wasn't for me you wouldn't have any money, or even know how to play poker for that matter, so don't get cute!" Broke and embarrassed, Gator thought, *since you sittin' here trying to fuckin' belittle me, I will find a way to get yo' ass back sooner or later.*

CHAPTER 16

As the small crowd dispersed from watching the classic battle between the two men, Deluxe turned to Gator. "Maybe you should think about taking a break for a while."

Gator frowned. "A break? Nigga, gangsta's don't take no breaks. The only time yo' ass will ever see me sittin' still is when I'm in a fuckin' coffin. Believe that."

But before Deluxe could reply, he was tapped on his shoulder from behind. When he turned around to see who it was, he was greeted by one of the most beautiful women that he'd seen in quite some time. She appeared to be around 5'6, a hundred and thirty five pounds, and had ass for days. Her beautiful tanned complexion said that she could've been from some sort of mixed decent, and her wavy light brown hair swung over her shoulders.

"Remember me, Mr. Deluxe?" the beautiful woman said. "You never did use the phone number I gave you."

Trying to remember where he'd seen her face before, Deluxe stared in awe for a few seconds. As he was about to respond, Gator beat him to the punch.

"Wait a minute, you that bitch, Suga right?" Gator asked. He looked her up and down and licked his lips. The all black tight fitting Chanel dress that was draped over her body accented every curve the voluptuous woman possessed.

"Yeah, that used to be what I went by. Now it's just Yasmin," she replied. "Oh, and not bitch either."

Deluxe continued to stare at the woman, who he now recognized. She looked completely different without the long blond wig. He immediately went into a trance thinking about the services she gave him that night.

"How did you get in the High Limit Gaming Room?" Gator asked. "You gamble?"

"No, I just have a few connections around here." Yasmin turned and winked at Bill, who quickly turned away.

"So, you workin' this spot now, huh? I thought you worked for Jimmy's greasy-ass over at Plan B," Gator inquired.

"Well, I decided that I'm much too classy to work for a weasel like Jimmy anymore. Plus, I can do me and keep it sexy in the process."

"Yeah fuck Jimmy!" Gator yelled.

Yasmin grabbed Deluxe by the arm, bringing him out of his thoughts. "You wanna finish what we started that night?" she whispered.

Deluxe looked at her beautiful almond shaped eyes. "Yasmin, what a beautiful name for such a beautiful woman. It fits you much better than Suga."

All Yasmin could do was blush as she dropped Deluxe's arm.

"Why don't we go up to the Iridescence restaurant to grab a bite to eat, and have a drink instead?" Deluxe suggested.

She smiled at his offer and nodded her head in approval. "I would like that."

Tryin' to show his nephew up, Gator grabbed Yasmin by the waist. He wasn't used to being ignored. "You should come and fuck wit' a real nigga."

"Obviously that's what I'm doin' if I'm leavin' with him and not you," Yasmin responded, yanking away from Gator's clammy hands. She was tired of him by this point.

Deluxe turned to his uncle and whispered in his ear. "Let this be the last time you try and disrespect me," he said, in a cold stern voice. "Don't let me have to embarrass yo' ass."

Seeing that he was finally able to get under his nephew's skin, Gator took another sip of champagne. He smiled at Deluxe as he and the exotic looking woman turned around to head for the exit. "I was just fuckin' wit' you Nephew. Look, forget about the money. Just take this before you leave." He reached in his pocket, and pulled out the Cabo ticket again. "We leave in two days."

Not wanting to argue in front of Yasmin, Deluxe grabbed the ticket from his uncle's hand, and walked away.

"I knew you would come around," Gator mumbled to himself.

• •

Deluxe and Yasmin shared small talk as they walked toward the luxury four diamond restaurant. The Iridescence was the cities newest and hottest spot. Everyone from high paid athletes like Rasheed Wallace and Rip Hamilton of the Detroit Pistons, to the cities elite like Mayor Kwame Kilpatrick and media mogul J. Thomas Pride, had all dined there.

Minutes later, Deluxe and Yasmin walked up to the entrance of the elegant eatery, where a friendly host greeted them. Because of his artistic display at the poker table, Deluxe was immediately treated as a high roller, and not subjected to waiting in the long line that wrapped around the corner.

After getting situated at a table which overlooked downtown Detroit, Deluxe told their server to bring over a bottle of Remy Martin Louis XIII Cognac. Even with all the money, he'd gained from working for Gator over the years, Deluxe wasn't known to splurge or flash his money, but in this case he felt it was needed.

Impressed by Deluxe's selection, Yasmin said with a sensual tone in her voice, "I see that you have exquisite taste, Daddy." Yasmin knew the best way to stroke a man's ego.

He smiled. "An exquisite drink for such an exquisite woman."

Yasmin blushed again when Deluxe recited the compliment to her. Although she was there to work, she was still a woman. A woman who liked being admired, and not just for her skills.

Seeing that she liked his flattering remark, Deluxe then asked her a question that she really wasn't expecting to hear. "Let me ask you somethin'. Why you still out here trickin' if you don't work at Plan B anymore?"

Yasmin looked out the window. She never wanted to live her life the way it was now, but without a mother or a father, Yasmin had to do whatever it took to take care of herself and her two siblings.

"Trust me, this ain't what I wanna be doin' with my life. I hate doin' this shit, and it's not something I'm proud of, but I really need the money," she replied solemnly. "At first I was doing it to put myself through school. Now I'm doing it to take care of my family."

"Why, you gotta a kid or something? Oh boy let me guess. Yo' lame-ass baby father don' ran out on you," Deluxe commented.

Yasmin laughed. "No, it's nothing like that. I have to take care of my little sisters, since my mother and father are not around anymore. They depend on me."

"That's deep. So where yo' folks at?"

As if it hurt to even talk about the subject, Yasmin spoke slowly. "My father died, and my mother might as well be dead 'cause she got strung out on crack a few years ago. Her crackhead ass has been in and out of our lives since then. Right now, me and my sisters live with my aunt, but I'm trying to save enough money so we can move out."

As she talked about her parents, Deluxe could sense the hurt and frustration that Yasmin had gone through when he looked in her eyes. He may have been a cold-blooded killer, but he sympathized with her. Besides, he'd lost majority of his family as well. He also couldn't believe how much they actually had in common.

"Wow, that's such a coincidence 'cause my folks are dead too. I was raised by my uncle."

"Really? So, was that your annoying uncle back in the gaming room?"

Deluxe shook his head. "Yeah unfortunately." He wanted to skip the current topic. "Now, gettin' back to yo' job choice. You way too beautiful to be out here fuckin' for money."

"Thanks, but a pretty face ain't gonna pay the bills."

"Yeah, well that may be true, but a pretty face can go out and find a better way to make money. Try modelin' or somethin'."

Slightly irritated by the way Deluxe was criticizing her, Yasmin barked, "Well since you're so damn smart. What do you do?"

Deluxe cleared his throat. "I'm in the Marines."

"Oh, really? That's surprising. It's good to see a hardworking black man who's not in the street."

Trying desperately to change the subject again, Deluxe finally poured two glasses of the fifteen hundred dollar Cognac. "Let's make a toast."

"A toast to what?"

Deluxe let out a huge grin. "A beautiful friendship with a beautiful woman."

Yasmin returned the gesture. "I'll toast to that."

After downing the smooth tasting liquor, Deluxe and Yasmin placed their food orders with the waiter. Deluxe ordered a prime NY strip steak, while Yasmin ordered grilled lemongrass-skewered prawns. The two new friends continued to share small talk with each other, while the executive chef prepared their meals.

Fifteen minutes passed before either of them realized it. While engulfed in their conversation, they barely even realized that the waiter had returned with the meals.

"How about we get out of here once dinner's over and fin-ish up what we started at Plan B," Yasmin suggested, as she stuffed a shrimp in her mouth.

Sensing that Yasmin was pressed by the clock, Deluxe replied, "No need to rush. I'ma pay you for the rest of the night. Relax."

All Yasmin could do was smile.

By the time they finished their food, the bottle of Louis XIII was almost finished, and both of them were a little on the tipsy side. Although she was feeling the effects of the alcohol, Yasmin suggested that it would be too dangerous for him to drive them somewhere in that condition.

Deluxe instantly agreed, and suggested that they get a room at the hotel. He figured that getting stopped at night by the Detroit PD was not a smart move. A DWB charge, Driving While Black, coupled with a DWI would definitely ensure that he met the wrong end of a Billy-club and maybe even a taser gun.

Preparing to leave the restaurant, Deluxe reached into his pocket and pulled out a large stack of hundred dollar bills. He quickly peeled off twenty of the bills and placed them in the black folder that was sitting on the table. As Deluxe motioned for the waiter to come to the table, Yasmin looked at the bundle and smiled. She wondered to herself how much more he had left. She also wanted to see how much of it she could possibly end up with by the end of the night.

Telling the waiter to have a good night, Deluxe, like a gentleman stuck out his arm toward Yasmin. "You ready pretty lady?"

Smiling at her newest mark, she grabbed his arm and replied, "Yes, I am." *I didn't even have to work too hard this time,* the seductress thought as she and Deluxe walked out.

● ●

After getting the key to an Executive Suite, Deluxe and Yasmin laughed and talked even more on the way to the elevator. Once inside, Yasmin didn't waste anytime brushing up against Deluxe with her large 36 C sized breasts, as she pressed the button to take them to the sixth floor. Sensing that Deluxe may have gotten aroused from the seductive move, she traced the outside of his ear with her tongue and whispered, "I'm sorry, I should've said excuse me. Will you forgive me?"

Turning to face her, Deluxe pulled Yasmin close to him and kissed her gently on her voluptuous lips. "Does that answer yo' question?"

Just as they were about to allow their tongues to dance around in each other mouth's, they were interrupted by the sounds of the elevator reaching their destination. Yasmin grabbed Deluxe's hand and led him down the hall to room 669. The perfect number for what was about to go down.

After entering the suite, Deluxe walked straight to the bathroom. He needed to relieve himself of all the liquor that they'd been drinking at the restaurant. After finally unleashing the waterfall of piss that seemed to last for days, Deluxe stepped out of the bathroom to a huge surprise. Yasmin stood in front of him with only her bra and panties on while R. Kelly's '*12 Play*' echoed from the radio.

"Damn baby. You got it all set up, huh?" he asked, looking around the room.

With the index finger that she'd just seductively removed from her mouth, she motioned for Deluxe to come to her.

Like a trained puppy, he walked toward the strikingly beautiful woman, and damn near panted. Once they stood face to face, Yasmin pushed him onto the plush bed and began to twist and wind her body to the beat of the music. She lip synced the words to the song as she began to unbutton the shirt that was draped on Deluxe's chiseled body. Lifting up the wife beater that fit snuggly around his chest, Yasmin started kissing Deluxe from his neck down to his firm chest. He began to breathe heavy as Yasmin explored his upper torso with her warm, wet tongue. With every tender kiss that she placed on his body, his heart beat faster and faster.

She worked her way down to his jeans which divulged his giant bulge in the center. Still looking up at him, Yasmin unfastened his belt and quickly unsnapped the button that stood between her and the love tool she was in search of.

"I almost forgot about this big dick," Yasmin said, with a slight grin.

She stood up and commanded Deluxe to take his pants off. Almost losing his cool, he jumped up and did exactly what he was told. Still impressed by what she saw, Yasmin softly began to rub the thick dick that was protruding out of his underwear.

"You ready for what I do best?" she asked.

Deluxe was in heaven, as he shook his head quickly. "Hell yeah."

With the ferociousness of a wild animal, Yasmin ripped his boxers off freeing his massive love muscle. She opened her mouth wide and began to engulf her throat with the thickening beast that Deluxe was blessed with. In a slow and steady pace, she licked the shaft of his dick with her tongue. Reaching the head of his rod, she wrapped her full lips around the pulsating head, and began her professional deep throat services. She bobbed harder and faster as Deluxe grabbed the back of her head to ensure that his dick and her tonsils would become closely acquainted. Feeling his penis jerk the more she sucked, Yasmin stood up and told Deluxe that she didn't want him to cum yet.

Taking off her bright red matching bra and thong set, she turned around. "I want you to fuck me hard, Daddy!"

Without hesitation, Deluxe rammed his python into the awaiting love tunnel that was dripping wet by this point. Working every inch of his dick into her pussy, which was drenched with her juices, Deluxe began to pound her from the back hard and steady. With each powerful blow that Deluxe delivered, Yasmin squealed in pleasure and said something that he could barely make out. Thoroughly enjoying the beat down that she was getting, Yasmin bounced her plump fat ass back on his dick with each and every pump that Deluxe delivered.

"Harder Daddy harder. Fuck me harder with this big dick," she screamed. "Oooh baby this dick is so fuckin' good," the sensual vixen moaned.

With his ego swelling, Deluxe asked, "You like this dick huh? You want daddy to fuck you harder?"

"Yes!"

Like a scene out of a Mr. Marcus porno flick, Deluxe took his horse like dick out of Yasmin and picked her up. Shocked at his display of strength, Yasmin wrapped her arms around his neck as he slowly lowered her back onto his intimidating pleasure stick. He bounced her up and down on his tool causing her to moan in ecstasy. The new position caused his penis to rub against her throbbing clit which was swelling with each pump. Unable to contain herself, Yasmin squeezed his neck tighter as she yelled, "Oh baby fuck me, I'm cummin' baby I'm cummin'!" Her amazingly addictive pussy coupled with the Louis XIII made Deluxe look like a thoroughbred stallion. Yasmin's body jerked and shook like a heroine fiend trying to quit cold turkey as her waterfalls erupted and ran down the shaft of Deluxe's magic stick. After unloading all of her juices, Yasmin jumped out of his arms and grabbed his dick and started stroking it up and down as she placed her new favorite lolli-pop in her mouth. Sucking and jerking his manhood like she'd been taught by Vanessa Del Río, Yasmin waited anxiously for the creamy white liquid that Deluxe was about to unleash on her throat. Rocking his hips back and forth as the cum started making its way from his sack to the head, Deluxe erupted like a volcano down Yasmin's esophagus and all over her lips. Not wanting to waste any of the tasty treat that was dancing around her mouth, Yasmin licked and sucked all of Deluxe until every drop had been robbed of his pleasure pump.

After the marathon episode, Deluxe collapsed on the bed feeling twenty pounds lighter. "Damn you got some good ass pussy," he said, as Yasmin laid on top of him and rubbed his chest.

"Well, my mother always told me to use what I got to get

what I want," she teased.

Unable to say anything and feeling overwhelmingly relieved, within minutes both of the wanna-be porn stars drifted off to sleep in each others arms.

CHAPTER 17

Jimmy the Greek was laid back in his Bentley Phantom talking to one of his Greek family member's up north, when his second line buzzed. It was Myth. "Let's make it quick, I'm on another call."

"Where should we meet?" Myth asked.

"Meet me at the Shock's game tonight. My box seats. Call before you get there."

"Are you serious? The fuckin' women?" Myth laughed.

"Yeah, so what's wrong with that?"

Not wanting to piss Jimmy off, Myth quickly changed his tune. "Oh, nothin'. It's just that I ain't never known a dude to go to a WNBA game before, that's all."

"Well, not that it's any of your business, but my box seats are year round mooley," Jimmy replied, just before hanging up.

After the call, Myth hoped that he hadn't fucked up his chances. On the other hand, he thought long and hard because with his potential new job, shit was really going to be blazing in the streets. Like Biggie always said, "Beef is when yo' moms ain't safe up in the streets." Since the jump off at Mylani's funeral, he'd been laying low and thinking of a way to destroy Gator once and for all. Not to mention Deluxe, whose cold killing style concerned him the most.

•••••••••••••••••••••••

Several hours later, Myth hopped in his Lexus LS and started the V-8 engine. Before pulling off, he decided to lean back in the driver's seat and spark up a blunt to help calm his nerves a little bit. Taking a hit of the chronic that he'd just gotten from Texas, Myth thought to himself that if everything went according to plan, it would be the night he would finally takeover the reigns of the city. After years of playing sidekick to Gator, he was finally going to get his chance to prove that he was the reason for the family's success. Although, Gator was the one who found Jimmy in the first place, it was Myth who had all the heart and the balls, which is what the Greek loved the most.

Stepping on the gas, Myth sped up interstate 75, so that he could meet Jimmy and make their plans official. Puffing on his blunt, he thought about how things were finally starting to come together for him. He would no longer be in the shadow of his one time best friend. Gator was falling fast and Myth planned on being there to watch him fall all the way down, and shoot him in the head if he tried to get back up.

Snapping out of his thoughts in enough time to take the exit to the Palace, Myth pulled out his phone to call the Greek to let him know that he was only minutes away. Receiving instructions from Jimmy on where to park his car, Myth pulled into the parking lot and did exactly as he was told. Minutes later, he was met by an attendant who escorted him up to the Vito Anthony Suites, where his meeting with Jimmy was taking place.

The Vito Anthony Suites were like nothing that Myth had ever seen before. He and Gator had the luxury of having numerous courtside tickets to the Pistons games before, but nothing like what Jimmy had laid out. The suite included a 60-inch plasma T.V., a fully stocked bar with bottles of Cristal and Louis XIV, a chef and a personal concierge to provide the guests with everything they needed.

"Myth, my good friend, come on in," the old man said, as Myth was escorted in the room by the same personal attendant from downstairs.

"Now, this is what I call livin' large," Myth said to Jimmy, as he stretched out his hand to shake his new partner's hand. "Oh, again sorry about that comment earlier. I didn't mean anythin' by it."

"Don't worry. Just enjoy yourself."

Myth finally smiled. "Thanks. I will."

"Where have you been hiding yourself over the past week or so?"

"I been up in Kalamazoo tryin' to get things together," Myth informed.

"Well fuck Gator. It time for that shit to end." Smiling from ear to ear, Jimmy wrapped his arm around Myth's neck. "You see that fucking mooley friend of yours could never appreciate the finer things like this in life. You can take a nigger out of the projects, but he'll still be a nigger." Jimmy spat, while laughing with the other men that stood in the room.

Looking at Myth, Jimmy continued. "That's why I wasn't surprised when you called, telling me you had a plan to get Gator back. It was smart of you to hand over the money and those keys you got from his dope house. Knowing that crater face mooley, he wouldn't have gone that route. "

Myth gritted his teeth at Jimmy's racial remarks, but he knew that he had to keep his temper in check. He'd been planning on making this power move since Kane's murder, and didn't need to fuck it up by losing focus on the big picture. Killing Gator and running South East Michigan's drug game was top priority. Ever since the night that Gator ordered the hit on his cousin, he knew that a bitter war was going to take place. Myth didn't have the connections or the street team that Gator had yet, but the one thing he did have now was Jimmy.

Myth had kept in contact with the Greek after the incident at Plan B. They both knew Gator's arrogance, disloyalty and disrespect would eventually get him killed and possibly the entire family locked up. However, Jimmy, nor his Greek family members, were going to stand by and let that happen. Once Kane was killed, Myth knew that he and Gator could never go back to being partners again. Robbing Gator's east side dope house for three hundred grand and his last thirteen keys was just one more thing that he'd done to get revenge. However, it was never his intentions for Momma Ruth to get killed, she just happened to be at the wrong place at the wrong time. Mylani was a different story. In honor of Kane, it was always in his plans for her to die. Kandi just happened to beat him to the punch.

"Oh, but listen, I've been meaning to ask you this for awhile now," Jimmy stated. "I heard there was an Alan's Shoe store bag in the car when they found that stripper girl Kandi's body. Now, you wouldn't happen to know anything about that would you? Especially since that was the same type of bag you brought to me inside the club that night?"

Myth swallowed hard. His original plan was to try and implicate Jimmy with the murder, but now he wished he could take it all back. He had to stay cool and play things off. "I heard that too, but trust me I didn't have anythin' to do wit' it. Shit, I would be a fool to ever mess wit' you like that. Actually, that girl Kandi was so foul it's no tellin' where she got the bag from."

Jimmy stared at Myth for what seemed like eternity. "It looks like someone was trying to set me up."

Myth shook his head. "I doubt it. It's probably just a coincidence. Everybody shops at that store."

"Well, just in case *someone* did try and associate me, I want it to be known that they did a bitch-ass job. I don't leave behind silly clues, and besides that's not my taste. If I wanted Gator to know that I had something to do with killing his woman, I would've mailed him one of her fucking arms or some shit."

Myth shook his head in agreement because he knew how brutal Jimmy could get.

Walking to the black leather chairs that where situated in the center of the suite, Jimmy told the personal concierge to leave, then called the meeting to order. "Okay, let's get down to business gentlemen."

Myth, and the other men in the room didn't waste anytime taking their seats. As he tried to get comfortable in the stiff wing back chair, Myth eyed each Greek quickly. The only familiar face was Sonny's, who stood by the bar and eyed him with an evil scowl.

Jimmy looked around the room at the crime syndicate that had gathered for the meeting. This was the first time since doing business with Gator that he felt good about introducing his family members to the person leading the drug game. He was always slightly embarrassed by Gator's flashy demeanor and cocky attitude.

"As most of you know, this family has taken some heavy financial losses recently due to one of our former members," Jimmy stated. "However, I assure each and every one of you that our little problem will be eliminated, and we'll be back to our number one mission, making money."

Before Jimmy could finish speaking he was interrupted by one of the men. In a typical New Jersey accent, the thin grey haired man asked, "And how long before this fucking mooley is dead and my product is back on these streets? I'm losing money every fucking day!"

Myth shifted in his seat. He hated the Greek's racial slurs with a passion.

A quiet murmur fell over the room as Jimmy continued. "I want to introduce you all to the man who'll be taking over the territory that was once controlled by Gator, and his name is Myth."

"What kind of assurance do I have that hundreds of our kilos will be able to be moved efficiently with this Myth person?"

another man yelled out.

Jimmy smiled at the blunt question. "Because, I have personally tested him, and his ability to follow orders. He's a good kid."

Turning to Sonny, who was still standing by the bar, Jimmy motioned for him to come over. Like the good flunky he was, Sonny walked over with a black duffle bag in hand. Giving the bag to Jimmy, Sonny looked at Myth and stared at him with the look of a hardened killer, and walked away.

That muthfucka always look like he gotta damn problem, Myth thought.

Jimmy walked over to Myth and handed him the duffle bag. "This is just a small taste of all the fucking money that we're gonna be making with this new partnership."

Myth grabbed the bag like a prized trophy, and then unzipped it before looking inside. His eyes lit up like light bulbs once he saw the ten kilos of cocaine and several stacks of money.

"You work for me now, so you can come on back from Kalamazoo. Trust me, no one is gonna be stupid enough to fuck with you now," Jimmy continued, as he stared at his new employee. "But let this be the first and last time I say this. If you ever try and fuck me or the family, I will personally give you, your girl and that precious son of yours, a slow and painful death."

Still looking at the pure white coke and the pile of cash that was placed throughout the bag, Myth slowly raised his head and nodded in approval at Jimmy's last statement. Ever since he'd gotten in the dope game he wanted to be the one who was calling the shots. Now it was his time to shine. Another look at all the money that was piled up in front of him quickly brought a smile across his face. Myth always felt that Gator never gave him his props as the major money maker of the family, especially after he got out of jail, so he was determined to set the record straight. Thinking of how he was going to rule the streets of the D, Myth finally zipped the duffle bag up, and leaned back in the leather chair. A chair that he'd finally gotten comfortable in.

CHAPTER 18

Arriving at Los Cabos International Airport, Gator stepped off the plane and was immediately met by the scorching one hundred and three degree weather. The exhausting six hour flight from Detroit to Mexico coupled with the brutally hot air added to Gator's growing anger. Knowing that this was possibly his last shot at getting back on, he felt extremely betrayed when Deluxe didn't show up at the airport that morning to take the trip with him. But for now, Gator needed to put his game face on and worry about his nephew's disloyalty later.

"They need to do somethin' 'bout this fuckin' airport. Why in the hell do we get on and off the plane outside?" Gator complained to himself. "They need some shit like we got in America."

As Gator walked toward the concourse, he continued to complain about the heat, which was unbearable by this point. The cream linen outfit that was now stuck to his body from all the sweat wasn't providing much relief either. After several complaints later, he finally stepped inside the terminal, providing an instant relief from the sun. Plus, seeing all of the beautiful tourists and Hispanic women walking around helped as well. Thoughts of how he would rather be up in some pussy than wiping pools of sweat from his blistering face entered his mind, and a slight smile finally appeared. However, that smile didn't last when the line to get through customs seemed longer than a football field.

"I can't wait to get outta this fuckin' place," he said to himself.

An hour and several frustrating moments later, Gator finally picked up his bag from the small and unorganized baggage claim, and walked toward the transportation area. Bypassing all the annoying timeshare stalkers, who were desperately trying to get his attention, Gator saw a tall muscular man in a suit holding a sign that read, "Mr. Donald Bumps," which immediately pissed him off even more. Gator knew the man was looking for him because he'd specifically informed Chico that he going by the name, Donald Trumps. For a moment, he thought the sign might've been referring to his bad skin.

"Is everybody in this fuckin' country a idiot," Gator said, to himself as he approached the man. "Yo', I think you lookin' fo' me."

"Hola Senor Bumps," the tall man responded.

Pissed off at how his fake name was blatantly wrong, Gator corrected his escort. "My name ain't no damn, Senor Bumps you got the shit all wrong. Man just call me Gator."

"Lo siento, I apologize Senor Gator." He laughed while escorting Gator to a white stretched Hummer.

"Well, it looks like Mr. Chico sent for me in style, huh?" The escort just shook his head and smiled. "Shit, is this what hell feels like?" Gator laughed, as he handed the escort his bag and stepped inside of the cool car.

"Oh yes, Senor Gator. It very hot here. Only rain few times in July," the escort replied, in his thick Mexican accent and broken english.

"Damn, no wonder some of y'all 'bout black as me."

After placing Gator's bag inside the trunk. He jumped in the driver's seat. "Cool drink inside, Senor Gator."

Once he got comfortable in the backseat, Gator helped himself to an ice cold Corona that was chilling in a bucket of ice. Twisting the cap, Gator shifted his thoughts to his meeting with Chico. With everything back in Detroit falling apart, he needed to leave Cabo with a plan to have Chico committing to front at least five keys to him. Keys that would put him back on top, back in the D. Keys that would allow him to regain some of the respect that he'd lost. Respect was something Gator had worked hard to get, and was an invaluable asset to him. So, without it, he was pretty much nothing.

As they pulled off and finally began making their way, Gator wondered where the ocean was. From what he'd seen so far, Cabo was nothing but mountains, cactus and dust. He wondered for a moment, if all the beautiful pictures he'd seen were just a facade.

Gator took a huge gulp of his beer. "Yo' Amigo. Where all the damn water at around here. All I see is dirt!"

"No problem, Senor Gator. We see water soon."

"Shit, I hope so. I ain't leave the D to be in no damn desert."

After what seemed like an eternity, they finally arrived at Chico's nine million dollar Italian style Villa located in Villa La Roca; Cabo's most exquisite cliffside estates. Gator had never seen anything so plush in his life. His house in Detroit looked like a matchbox compared to Chico's beachfront mansion. As the car came to a complete stop, Gator saw hundreds of grounds keepers walking around manicuring what looked to be an already perfected lawn.

Gator didn't even wait for his escort to open the door before he jumped out. He looked around at the beautiful scenery and thought to himself, this was the way he should be living.

"Yeah, I need to hurry up and get back on, so I can get me a house out this muthafucka. Damn!"

"I bring your bag later. Please follow me, Senor," his escort announced, as he led Gator around the villa to the pool area.

Gator strutted behind the tall man as they walked toward the beautiful infinity style swimming pool in the back of the mansion. The closer he got, Gator couldn't believe how breath taking the view of the Pacific Ocean was. The crystal blue water was just like looking at a postcard. He also couldn't believe how many gorgeous women Chico had prancing around wearing tiny thong bikini's, or nothing at all. For a second, Gator thought he was at one of the Playboy Mansion's famous pool parties. He could hardly control himself as he walked past one stunning woman after another. Now he really was in heaven.

Sitting on an all white lawn chair, Chico motioned for the escort to take Gator to the bar that was sitting poolside. As the two men walked up, Gator was handed a mix drink by a beautiful naked woman with reddish colored hair.

"Compliments of Senor Ramos," the woman informed.

"What else is on the house?" Gator asked smartly, as he winked at the woman before he and the escort walked over to where Chico sat.

Chico was stuffing money into an automatic counter when the escort announced, "Senor Ramos, this is Senor Gator."

Nodding his head, Chico never took his eyes off the money

to acknowledge Gator's presence and continued to stuff the machine. Gator immediately took Chico's lack of eye contact as a sign of disrespect. Under normal circumstances, he would've let his ego and arrogance get the best of him, but he knew that he had to keep a cool head in order to get the deal done. Not to mention, he was in foreign territory. After stuffing and watching the last stack of money fly through the machine, Chico finally stood up to greet his guest.

Chico was a short slender man with a fly sense of style that even made Gator envious. He wore an all white linen short set with a six hundred dollar pair of Roberto Cavalli sandals, and large Versace glasses. His pecan colored skin tone and long curly black hair, gave him an exotic model look that Gator wished he had.

"Welcome to my home Gator. It's great to see you again. I do apologize for the inconvenience of waiting. Like you, I am a business man and I don't like to wait," the small commanding man informed, in a perfect english accent. He reached out to shake Gator's hand. "Please have a seat."

"Thanks, Chico."

As soon as Gator sat down on one of the expensive looking lawn chairs, Chico motioned for one of the girls to come over. Seconds later, a short thick woman with the look of a young Selma Hayek, strutted over to Gator and sat on his lap. She was wearing a red jeweled thong bikini that showed off her round ass and perky

38 D's. The woman Chico called, Carmen immediately shoved her

tongue down Gator's throat and began to kiss him and rub on his

dick, which was now beginning to bulge through his pants.

"Damn, I can get used to this shit", Gator said, as Carmen

finally gave his tongue a break. She rose from his lap and walked

away.

Laughing at the look on Gator's face, Chico said, "It's more

where that came from my friend. Just wanted to show you what's

in store after the deal is done."

"That's what the fuck I'm talkin' bout," Gator said excit-

edly. "Shit, it look like Cabo is the place where I need to be. How

much houses runnin' over this muthafucka?"

"Well, before you make plans to leave Detroit, let's discuss

the reason why you're here."

At that moment, Gator began to sweat a little harder under

the blazing Mexico sun. He knew that he didn't have anywhere

near the money that was needed to make the deal happen. When

the two men last talked, they had agreed that Gator would wire him

two hundred thousand dollars to a secure bank account up front.

However, since his last dope house was hit, Gator only had four

thousand dollars left to his name. Every time they talked on the

phone, Chico made it very clear to him that he was about business and had no tolerance for bullshit, so Gator was taking a huge risk.

"Wait, before we start, how's that beautiful girl I saw you with last year. I forget her name," Chico said.

Gator knew he was referring to Mylani, and really didn't want to answer. "She not wit' me anymore."

"Oh, let me guess. You got caught with your dick in another piece of pussy, huh? Probably with a beautiful woman like Carmen."

Deciding not to tell Chico his business, Gator agreed. Besides, he didn't want his possible new connect to think that he had beef back home. "Yeah man she dumped my ass big time."

"I knew it. Anyway, here's the way that I do business Gator. I deal with you and only you. No exceptions. I'll also only provide you with a certain quantity on a monthly basis. Too much could be risky." Removing his glasses so that Gator could finally see his cold dark eyes, Chico continued. "Now, understand this. I never accept excuses. They're for fools and women, not good businessmen. Now, if you're ready to do business, I can have my private jet escort you back to Detroit by the end of the night after we're done celebrating our deal. Oh, and don't worry about U.S. Customs my friend. That's all taken care of. You American's can be bought with money so easy."

"With all due respect Chico, I wouldn't be here if I wasn't

ready to do business," Gator replied, in a matter of fact tone.

"Great, that's what I like to hear." Turning to one of his workers, Chico said, "Ven aqui."

A few seconds later, another tall burly man standing around six foot three came over to Chico and handed him a large Louis Vuitton suitcase. When Chico opened the expensive luggage, Gator's eyes widened when he saw the numerous kilos of cocaine that were tightly packed inside. He hadn't had a hit since leaving Detroit, so the highly addictive drug was definitely calling his name.

Damn, I hope I can get a sample, Gator thought.

"I don't doubt that you're capable of moving as much as you say you can my friend, but I like to start my new business partners out with a small amount to see exactly what they can do. This amount is smaller than the twenty keys we originally spoke about," Chico said to him, while zipping the suitcase back up.

Gator hated to see the coke disappear. "How much is it then?"

"This here my friend is ten kilos of Colombia's purest and most raw cocaine," Chico replied, patting the bag. He then gave Gator a stern look. "So, now that you've seen what I have for you. What do you have for me? You were supposed to wire the money, right?"

Sweating harder than a hooker in church by this point, Gator felt a lump begin to form in his throat. "Umm, that's what I need to talk to you about. Right now, I'm not exactly prepared to take ten kilos. I ran into some setbacks and…"

Before Gator could finish his sentence, Chico bluntly interrupted him. "I just told you excuses are for fools and women, so what do I look like to you? I don't fuck around when it comes to my time or my money, and you're wasting both at this point!"

"No, honestly I'm not. I thought by me flyin' all the way over here, it would show you that I mean business."

"So, answer this. How many keys do you want?"

Gator wiped his head. "Actually I was hopin' that you could front me at least five keys for right now. I promise on my mother's life, I'll have yo' money in no time. I'm telling you. I got a good name for business back in Detroit. It's nothin' for me to move that lil' bit of shit."

"On your mother's life, huh?" Chico uttered suspiciously. He seemed furious as his left eye twitched out of control. "You have a lot of balls asking me to front you some shit with no money."

Seeing that something was about to pop off, Gator quickly tried to talk his way out of it. He let Chico know that if five wasn't possible, he would take an even smaller quantity just to get back on his feet, but it wasn't working. Thinking that Gator was full of shit, and not the boss he'd claimed to be, Chico called his goons over to deal with the situation.

Within moments, three big Mexican men swarmed Gator and began to attack him. Two of the goons stretched Gator out while the third one pounded his face with multiple right and left hooks. He then punched Gator numerous times in the stomach. Every time he would fall to the ground, the goons would pick him back up, and inflict even more pain. The worse was when all three goons held a stomping contest, kicking every part of his body, especially his ribcage.

Chico whistled a few minutes later, bringing an end to the massive beating.

Barely able to speak, Gator pleaded nervously one last time. "Chico...please. I swear. I'm a good...guy. I even got about...four grand back at home that I can send to...you. That should be good for somethin'...right? "

Chico walked over to Gator, who was on the ground bleeding like a wounded animal and barely conscious. "You just don't get it, huh? Normally, I would've had your dick cut off and thrown in the ocean, or better yet I would've killed your black ugly ass by now, but today is my daughter's birthday, so I'm trying to be nice. Four thousand couldn't even buy you a night with one of my girls, let alone buy any of my shit."

Losing all hope, Gator hung his head in defeat. His only shot at getting back on top in the city that he once ruled with an iron fist had slipped through his hands. He'd lost his mother, fiancé, unborn child, best friend, and all of the money he had to his name. In less than a month's time, everything he'd worked so hard for was gone. The only thing Gator had left was Deluxe, but the way things were going now, even that relationship was unpredictable.

Turning to his goons, Chico demanded something in his native tongue before walking away. Without looking up at the man who'd just killed his hopes, the last thing Gator remembered was being kicked several more times before the lights finally went out for good.

CHAPTER 19

Days passed and life had become more pleasing for Deluxe as he and Yasmin found themselves spending more and more time together. Since the night at the casino, they'd spent every moment exploring one another's sexual pleasures, and quickly found out that they both had high sex drives. Both were getting used to being with someone who wanted to fuck, and they would spend hours going at it like two wild animals.

Their sexual escapades frequently consisted of toys and gadgets that would make the most skilled porn star envious. More importantly, Deluxe loved the fact that his new lover, loved the taste of his cum. Every chance that Yasmin got, she was trying to slurp up his bodily fluids, sending Deluxe into complete ecstasy each and every time. She also had a fetish for allowing him to fuck her in the ass, which by this point really seemed to have him wide open. With all the sex and a wonderful personality to match, Deluxe was quickly becoming attached to the beautiful young woman, and could care less who knew.

Just like any other day, Deluxe was looking forward to the

afternoon with Yasmin. To show his appreciation for all the good sex, he'd sent her to the hair salon to get a full day of beauty. Katt Williams was in town for the weekend, and he was planning on taking her to the comedy show at the Fox Theatre later on that evening. Even though Yasmin had the means to get her hair and nails done at a nicer spot, she loved going to Turning Headz Salon on East 7 Mile, right in the hood. She said that hood beauticians knew how to do hair better than the uppity bitches at the nicer salons, but Deluxe could've cared less either way. As long as she was happy that's all that mattered.

Stepping out of Turning Headz looking like one of the beauties off of America's Next Top Model, Yasmin smiled as Deluxe jumped out of the rental car to greet her with a huge hug. He had exchanged the Hyundai for a pearl white Escalade, just so Yasmin could ride around town in style. As they embraced, Yasmin didn't waste anytime slipping her tongue in his mouth. The two kissed like they were trying to tickle each other's tonsils with their tongues. Everyone who walked by looked at the pair like they needed to get a room, and more than likely, that was their next destination.

After the couple's tongue wrestling session ended, they both smiled at each other then walked toward the truck. However, Deluxe stopped in mid stride when he saw a familiar face walking across the street. A face that he hadn't seen since Mylani's funeral. He was completely startled. It was Myth.

Myth must've been just as surprised to see Deluxe, because once the two warriors made eye contact, they both looked like they'd seen a ghost. Oblivious to what was going on, Yasmin kept walking to the truck, but in one smooth motion, Deluxe pushed her out the way. Quickly, he pulled out his Glock and jumped behind the rental. Full of rage at seeing Deluxe's face, Myth pulled out his gun as well, and began shooting in the rental car's direction before taking cover himself. The two one time friends exchanged rapid gun fire back and forth sending everyone in the salon and on the street corner ducking for cover.

A woman who was about to walk out of the shoe store next door screamed, as she tried to shield her baby from the bullets that were recklessly flying in every direction. Peeking from around the truck, Deluxe caught a slight glimpse of Myth's fitted Detroit Tiger's hat. He immediately took aim, sending a few shots toward his head. Surprisingly he missed.

"Fuck," Deluxe mouthed to himself. He wasn't used to missing his target whatsoever.

Even though Myth wasn't as skilled as Deluxe when it came to the gun play, the rapid pace at which he sent his numerous hollow tips caused Deluxe to remain in hiding.

Knowing that his bullets were running low, Deluxe tried to think of how he was going to make it out of this shit alive. Luckily, Yasmin had managed to crawl back into the salon after Deluxe pushed her out of the way. Not knowing Myth's intentions, Deluxe desperately wanted to make it inside to try and protect her just in case Myth pulled a Rambo move. Peeking around the left side of the truck again, Deluxe saw Myth kneeling behind a silver Dodge Charger that was riddled with bullets. As if they were trying to figure out each others next move, they both kept taking quick looks to see what the other was doing.

Shit, that nigga gotta be low on bullets too, Deluxe thought. *Fuck it, it's now or never.*

Deciding to make a bold run for the door, Deluxe sent a couple more bullets in Myth's direction, as he jumped from behind the truck and dove toward the salon's entrance. Feeling like this was his time to shine, Myth stood up and let off several more rounds as Deluxe dove through the opening. Barely missing Deluxe with one of the slugs from his .45, Myth only managed to hit the salon's glass door, which instantly shattered.

Once inside, Deluxe ordered everyone in the salon to shut the fuck up and stay down. He quickly ran over to the side window that was closest to the street, and started firing in Myth's direction, again with the last few bullets he had. Unable to get out of the way fast enough, Myth caught two slugs in his chest, causing his body to be slung to the ground underneath the destroyed Charger.

Thinking that he'd finally gotten rid of the person who he believed was really behind Mylani's death, Deluxe let out a quick sigh of relief before running outside to put a couple more hot ones in Myth's head. He had to make sure he'd finished the job.

Deluxe looked around to see if anyone was crazy enough to be standing outside before he headed straight for the Charger that was now smoking as a result of the numerous bullet holes. Surprisingly, when Deluxe walked to where he saw Myth fall, he was stunned at what was there. Absolutely nothing.

"Shit, that muthafucka must've had a vest on. I know I hit his bitch- ass with two to the chest," he said to himself, looking in every direction.

There was no sign of Myth anywhere, and the approaching sounds of sirens caused Deluxe to quickly snap out of his trance and head for the salon to make sure that Yasmin was okay. Stepping on the shattered glass that was now covering the entire floor, Deluxe ran over to the chair that she was hiding behind, and kneeled down.

"Yasmin baby come on. We gotta get the fuck up outta here!" he yelled as he tried to help her up.

Crying uncontrollably, Yasmin screamed, "I'm not going

anywhere with you until you tell me what in the hell is going on. What is all this shit about?"

"Look, the muthafuckin' cops will be here in a minute. I ain't got time to be standin' here arguin'. Go get in the fuckin' car!" Deluxe yelled, pulling Yasmin by her trembling arm.

Yasmin had lived in Detroit her entire life, but this was the first time she'd ever been face to face with how her city got down. In a matter of seconds, she'd seen her entire life flash before her eyes, making the entire incident too much to handle. All she could think about were her two younger sisters having to raise themselves, and that couldn't happen. Yasmin needed to know who the fuck Deluxe really was, and what he was involved in.

In a shaken voice, Yasmin screamed at Deluxe and began hitting him on his arms as he peeled off down 7 Mile. "Tell me what the fuck is going on Deluxe!" Yasmine yelled, as tears ran down her cheeks.

"Look, I know you upset, but you gotta calm down."

"How in the hell am I supposed to calm down when all I know is one minute we're kissing, and the next minute somebody is trying to blow our fucking head off!"

Yasmin wiped the overflowing tears with the back of her hand before getting into his shit once again. "If I would've known that you were some type of damn gangsta, I would've never fucked with you. I don't want no parts of this shit. I thought your ass was supposed to be in the military!"

"I am," Deluxe replied, in his defense.

"Well if that's the case, why are people shooting at you? I thought the damn war was overseas?"

Instead of another lame excuse or a lie, he chose to remain quiet as Yasmin continued on her own war path. "If it's one thing I can't stand, it's a fucking liar."

Deluxe sat emotionless for a minute and looked straight ahead as he tried to get away from the east side, and back to safer territory. Seeing that Yasmin was terrified and that he could've gotten her killed over some bullshit, Deluxe began to feel guilty. He'd hoped that Yasmin would never have to know about this part of his life, but now it was no longer a secret. Whenever she would ask him when he was going back to the military, Deluxe would change the subject, or tell her he had tons of leave to use. But now it was time to clear the air. He knew he owed her an explanation. After all, Myth had almost ended both of their lives.

"The least you can do is answer me damn it!" Yasmin screamed.

Feeling that they were far enough away, Deluxe decided to pull the truck over so he could try and explain to Yasmin what was going on. After putting her life in danger, she deserved that much.

He just hoped that she wouldn't judge him or even worse, end the beginning of a good thing.

"Look Yasmin, we haven't even known each other that long, but you know I would never do anythin' to hurt you, right?"

She shook her head slightly. "Yeah, go on."

"Well, because of some bad business deals that my uncle has, now I'm a target," Deluxe explained, hoping to find some sympathy.

"What does your uncle's business deals have to do with you? Are you involved in drugs or something? 'Cause if you are, I told you, I can't handle this shit. My mother is a crack head. Do you think I wanna be around drugs!"

"I'm not into drugs. It's just that my uncle has made a lot of enemies in his line of work, and sometimes the best way to get at a person is to hurt the ones closest to them," Deluxe tried to explain.

Despite what he was saying, Yasmin kept asking questions.

"If you're not involved with drugs, then why would you be carrying around a gun and shooting at people? And you had the nerve to tell me that my line of work is dangerous, and that I need to get out of the game. You need to take your own damn advice!" she screamed, trying to slap him across the face in the process.

Deluxe gritted his teeth and grabbed Yasmin by the arms. Trying to keep his composure, he thought about how to get rid of

Myth, and not get killed in the process. "Look Yasmin, I'm not involved in the same things that my uncle is involved in. But at the same time I'm going to do everythin' in my power to protect myself. Truthfully, I used to work wit' my uncle but not in the way that you thinkin'. I took care of small problems for him, but all of that shit has come to a end. I'm actually no longer fuckin' wit' him like that. Meaning, I'm no longer in the game at all baby girl, so don't worry, you can trust me."

"What about the military? Did you lie about that?"

He shook his head. "Well, right now I guess you can say I was in the Marine Corps. I took leave a few weeks ago, but then got wrapped up in a lot of my uncle's shit and never went back. By now I'm sure they've considered me going AWOL, which ultimately means a dishonorable discharge."

Deluxe wrapped his arms around Yasmin to try and calm her down. He lifted her head and wiped her face that was now beet red, and covered in tears. Kissing her on the forehead, Deluxe said, "I swear to you baby girl, I'm not gonna let anythin' happen to you either. You gotta trust me."

Feeling safe in his arms, Yasmin finally started to calm down. "I'm not worried about me Deluxe, I'm worried about you. What am I gonna do if that crazy nigga doesn't miss the next time?"

Realizing just how lucky he was to be alive, Deluxe thought to himself that he was going to have to kill Myth, and soon. He definitely didn't want to take the chance on there being a next time.

Taking a deep breath he said, "Don't even think like that, I'ma be a'ight. Come on let me get you home, so you can get changed. Let's not let this shit ruin our night."

Pulling the truck back into traffic, Deluxe jumped on the Lodge Freeway and headed toward Southfield to Yasmin's aunt's house. However, the whole ride there all he could think about was killing Myth.

You wanna play big boy games nigga. We'll see how you like this shit, he thought as he stepped on the gas.

CHAPTER 20

Shit can't get no worse than this, Gator thought to himself as he sat on the plane holding his aching left side and waiting for the 747 jet to take off. He couldn't get back to Detroit fast enough. The cheap ten-dollar looking sunglasses he'd found in the men's bathroom right before boarding the plane, tried to hide his badly beaten face. He began to shake his head as thoughts of waking up inside a run-down Mexican jail cell the day before, entered his mind. Luckily Gator, who was barely conscious, had been found by two Mexican police officers in San Jose, a small town eighteen miles from Cabo San Lucas. Thinking he was just another drunk American tourist, who'd drifted on the wrong side of town, the police decided to throw him in jail so he could sober up. Little did they know, he was far from being intoxicated. The verge of death, was more like it.

Apparently, Chico's goons had decided to leave him in the rough section of San Jose, hoping a few locals would finish the job by robbing him or even worse, taking his life. They'd even thrown Gator's bag on the ground with him to attract the criminals swarming around the neighborhood. Obviously, things didn't work out as planned.

However, just like Chico's goons, the police who Gator thought were the good guys ended up being just as shady. Even after pleading to them that he was never drunk, all the money he had in his bag, had to be given to the crooked police officers just so they would let him out, which by the way took two days of convincing. For some reason, they thought Gator had family with him, who was willing to give them more. Gator also had to come up off the platinum Jesus piece that he cherished, cell phone, the two outfits he'd packed, and a comfortable pair of Ferragamo shoes. The only things they allowed him to keep were his passport, plane ticket, and the key to his car, which by far were the most important items. Wanting to get out of Mexico alive, Gator was willing to give up whatever it took in order to see American soil again. Even if it meant walking on the plane butt naked.

Taking the two extra strength Tylenol pills he'd gotten from the flight attendant, Gator drifted off to sleep minutes later thinking about how he was going to fuck Deluxe up for not being there for him when he got home.

• •

Elated to finally touch down on U.S. grounds, Gator damn near ran to his Benz after getting off the plane, then jumped inside and took off. He used the hundred dollar bill that he always left in his car's glove compartment for emergencies to pay the parking bill. He then took out something else that he used in desperate circumstances…his spare cell phone. Gator wasn't sure if he'd received any calls on his main cell phone, but most of the time when he didn't answer, people always called the spare. However, after looking at the small flip phone which showed no missed calls, it only threw fuel on his already blazing temper.

"That muthafucka Deluxe just don't give a fuck no more, huh? I could be fuckin' dead somewhere," Gator said to himself. "He didn't even have the nerve to call and apologize for not showing up. That's a'ight I'ma fix his bitch-ass once and for all." He pressed the gas pedal a little harder, speeding up I-96 on his way home. "As a matter of fact, let me call this muthafucka right now!"

Gator dialed Deluxe' number, but the call was sent straight to his voicemail, which pissed Gator off even more. The only family that he had left was now ignoring him. Within the next few minutes, he tried calling Deluxe a couple more times, but just like before each call got sent directly to the voicemail. Gator couldn't understand how the man he'd raised like a son could just turn his back on him without a second thought.

Unable to contain his anger any longer, Gator called Deluxe again, but this time decided to leave a message. "Deluxe,

look nigga why the fuck you actin' like a bitch and ain't answerin'
the muthafuckin' phone? First you take the ticket for Cabo, and
don't show up, now this. I'ma need you to call me back ASAP
nigga!"

The twenty-minute ride from the airport to his house
seemed to take forever. Now more than ever, he was feigning for a
hit of that white horse, and couldn't wait to be with his new best
friend. After punching in the key code for the front gate, Gator
quickly pulled into his garage and jumped out the car slamming the
door in the process. If his vehicle would've been anything other
than luxury, the windows would've probably shattered from the
force that he used.

Using the spare key in the garage, he walked into the house
and was getting ready to call out Mylani's name, but had to stop
himself. He was so used to her being there whenever he came
home from out of town. For some strange reason, he could even
still smell the Chanel Chance perfume that she used to wear.

"Damn I still can't believe she's gone. What the fuck am I
gonna do?" he asked himself.

Picking up a picture that he and Mylani had taken recently,
Gator broke down and cried like a baby. For the first time since all
this shit went down, Gator knew that he was in this fight all alone.

Knowing that he would never make love to his fiancé

again, see their unborn child, or taste his mother's cooking, Gator

lost it. He started throwing everything in sight, including the ex-

pensive paintings that Mylani hand picked, and her crystal figurine

collection that she cherished. After looking at his reflection in a

mirror, Gator knew that he was losing it. Along with a badly

bruised face, his hair hadn't been cut in over a week, and he still

had on the same three-day old bloody linen outfit. Not to mention

his body odor reeked. If it were three things that Gator never went

without, it was a shower, a fresh cut, and a brand new outfit, so the

new look was way out of his character. Along with a neat appear-

ance, everything in his life was gone except his name in the streets,

but the way things were going around town, he wasn't even sure if

that would bring the fear it once held. Gator was definitely headed

toward rock bottom.

Feeling an overwhelming amount of pain to his side, along

with a huge amount of stress, Gator felt that enough was enough.

Stumbling into his office, he ran behind his desk, opened the bot-

tom drawer and started throwing everything out onto the floor.

That is until he found what his heart was begging for…that perfect

storm, which is what he liked to call it.

He took the plastic bag that held his white lover and looked

at it, before dumping his last ounce all over the desk. He didn't

care that his face was still swollen from the ass whoopin' he'd gotten just two days ago. The only thing that was on his mind was seeing how much he could snort. Normally, Gator took the time to line out his hit, but not on this occasion. Looking up at his picture of Tony Montana on the wall, he smiled before shoving his face into the pile that he'd formed. Gator kept his face down until he'd snorted and licked every crumb of coke up off his desk. Not even the blood that was oozing out of his nose stopped him from enjoying the high that took place.

The cocaine instantly made Gator forget his pain. After finally sitting up, he then decided to pull out another drawer which contained his other best friend...a bottle of Hennessey. He took the liquor straight to the head, and didn't stop until the liquor was barely gone. Gator sat at his desk getting wasted, all along thinking about how fucked up his life was at the moment. He was dead broke and losing his grip on Detroit's drug game because of the two men he trusted the most. The more Gator thought about how Deluxe and Myth were disrespecting him, the more pissed off he became. The liquor mixed with the coke only fueled Gator's anger. He leaned back in his chair and decided that it was time to go all out. Reaching into another desk drawer, he grabbed his Desert Eagle. Looking at the gun like a piece of pussy, he licked his white coated lips and said, "Niggas that play pussy get fucked!"

Gator jumped up causing his chair to flip over in the

process. Gulping down the last bit of the Henny, he threw the bottle up against the wall causing it to shatter all over the expensive carpet that covered the floor. On a mission to find his disloyal family, Gator grabbed his fully loaded gun and headed straight for the door.

CHAPTER 21

Gator hopped in his Benz and started speeding out the driveway thinking of places where he could possibly find his nephew, or maybe even Myth. On the way down the street, he flipped open his cell phone to call Deluxe again, and like all the other times, the call was sent straight to voicemail. He couldn't believe Deluxe was treating him like some regular nigga off the street. Flying into a rage, Gator left him another voicemail.

"Nigga, I been callin' yo' ass for a minute now!" Gator hollered into the phone. "Muthafucka, if you hidin' somewhere, come the fuck out!"

Throwing the phone down on the floor, Gator pressed on the gas as he tried to figure out where his nephew could be. Still in need of answers and most of all some money, he headed to the west side. He had a small dope house on Kendall and Wyoming that he used to use from time to time for emergencies, and hoped that a few of the local crackheads might've seen one of the men. If not, he wasn't gonna stop until he found somebody who had.

Gator jumped off on Schoolcraft and headed toward the

house at full speed. When Deluxe still hadn't returned his phone call, it caused him to grow angrier by the minute as he turned onto Wyoming.

"Shit, while I'm at the spot, I might be able to find a lil' leftover white horse for myself," he said out loud, as he crept down the street. As Gator got closer, he saw a bunch of niggas running in and out of the house like someone was giving shit away for free.

"What the fuck is goin' on over here? Who the fuck are these niggas?" he wondered, as he stopped his car and shoved it in park.

Seeing money being made at one of his spots when he didn't even have anything to sell, Gator grabbed his burner and jumped out of his car. Still feeling like he was the king of the streets, he walked up to one of the young looking nigga's who looked like he was running shit.

Not recognizing who Gator was, the young guy asked, "What you need?"

"What I need?" Gator asked offended. "Who the fuck are you?" he spat, approaching the young hustler.

"Nigga, I'm Premo, and unless you wanna…" Premo attempted to reply when Gator pulled his Desert Eagle out and shoved it into his side.

Laughing at how he got the drop on the young boy, Gator

replied, "Unless I wanna what? Now you bitch-ass nigga? I been waitin' to get at yo' ass for a minute now, Mr. Premo."

"Yo' I'on think you know who's spot you runnin' up on like this!" Premo told him, as Gator motioned for him to walk around the side of the house.

Damn I ain't been off my grind that long for this lil nigga not to know that this is my shit. "What the fuck does that supposed to mean? This my spot, muthafucka!"

Premo looked at Gator like he was definitely on some of the shit that was being sold.

"Nigga, you must don't know who the fuck I am. I'm Gator. King of these muthafuckin' streets!"

Premo's eyes widened. "Damn, Gator I ain't even recognize yo' black ass. You over here lookin' like one of these muthafuckin' fiends I'm servin' and shit."

Gator shoved his gun into Premo's side even harder. "I'ma show you a muthafuckin' fiend nigga. Run me yo' shit!"

"A'ight, calm the fuck down. Myth gon' come lookin' fo' yo' ass fo' this shit!"

Gator couldn't believe what he'd just heard. "What the fuck did you say?"

"I said Myth gon' come lookin' fo' yo' ass if you take my shit. He don't fuck around."

"What the hell is that supposed to mean? Myth don't run shit around here!"

Premo smiled. "Well, I don't know where yo' ass been, but he do run shit around town now. Hell, he even ran me outta business. I work fo' his ass now."

The news that Myth was now running the dope house that he'd built was still hard for Gator to believe. His mind started racing and all he could think about now was putting a bullet in Myth's head. Here he was struggling to get back on, and Myth had taken over one of his old spots. To make matters worse, it looked like the spot wasn't hurting for business either. Gator let his arm down releasing the death grip that he held Premo with.

Premo knew that he had fucked Gator up with what he'd just told him. "Yeah nigga, the word around town is that you don' fell the fuck off and shit. Myth the man in the D now," Premo said, rubbing the news in. "You out here tryna rob niggas while Myth makin' money. What a shame."

"So, who is Myth's connect? Where he gettin' his shit from?"

"Why, what difference do it make nigga? All you need to know is that he took over yo' shit."

Gator lifted the gun again. "Answer the damn question, muthafucka!"

"A'ight man. It's Jimmy. Jimmy is his connect."

Gator felt betrayed now more than ever. "I can't believe this shit," he said, putting the gun down slightly.

"Well, believe it. Man what the hell is up wit' y'all? First you fall off, now yo' nephew is out here all in love wit' that hoe. I mean damn, don't his ass know that he fuckin' a cop's daughter. Since when y'all start hangin' out wit' cop families and shit."

Gator's face frowned. "A cop's daughter? "What the fuck you talkin' bout? What cop?"

Laughing at Gator in his face, Premo answered, "Detective Hughes nigga! That bitch Suga is his daughter."

Gator looked puzzled.

"Don't tell me, yo' ass ain't know either? Man, I thought y'all niggas was supposed to be the shit around town. Instead, y'all seem dumb as a muthafucka to me. No wonder Myth took over. Shit, I even heard Myth almost tapped yo' nephew's ass durin' that shoot out the other day. And that muthafucka supposed to be some type of assassin." Premo laughed again.

Not finding anything funny about what was being said, Gator put the gun to Premo's head. "Do you see somethin' funny muthafucka? As a matter of fact, empty yo' damn pockets nigga!"

Realizing that he was dealing with a desperate man, Premo reached in his pocket, and pulled out the stack of money that he'd been collecting all day.

"Yeah bitch, gimmie all yo' muthafuckin' bread nigga," Gator told Premo, as he handed him what he had. "Run me yo' stash too!" Gator demanded.

"We ain't re-upped yet."

"Don't fuckin' play wit' me!" Gator said angrily. "You gon' make me bust yo' muthafuckin' shit wide open!"

"Do what the fuck you gotta do then."

Not wanting to waste anymore time fucking with Premo, Gator hit the young hustler with the butt of his gun causing the him to fall to the ground, holding the back of his head.

"Yo' ass is as good as dead nigga!" Premo yelled, as Gator hopped back in his whip even more fucked up than he was before.

• • • • • • • • • • • • • • • • • • • •

The search for Deluxe was on. Gator figured the best place to look for him first was Momma Ruth's house. Speeding through town like a professional drag racer, it didn't take long for him to get to the west side of town. Just as he thought, Gator saw a Escalade parked in the driveway, which couldn't have belonged to anyone else but Deluxe.

"What the fuck happened to that Hyundai," Gator asked out

loud, as he pulled up behind the truck and placed his car in park. He quickly hopped out and slammed the door in the process. Gator was so angry he didn't even notice the bullet holes that were taking over Deluxe's rental.

This nigga is laid up over here chillin' in my momma's shit when I need his ass out here handlin' fuckin' business, Gator thought as he rushed up the stairs to the door. Without knocking, or even using the spare key that was always kept in Momma Ruth's flower bed, Gator kicked in the door and immediately started screaming Deluxe's name.

"Deluxe, where the fuck you at nigga?" Gator hollered, as he walked through the kitchen and toward the basement. "I know you in here!"

Deluxe was caught off guard as he heard Gator upstairs cursing and yelling at the top of his lungs. He knew it was only a matter of time before he would have to face his uncle, and tell him that he was done, once and for all. He was tired of playing Gator's games, especially now that his own life had almost been taken away. Before Deluxe could make it upstairs, Gator opened the basement door forcefully, and began running down the stairs.

Deluxe and Gator finally stood face to face for the first time since the casino incident. He looked at Deluxe with hatred in his bloodshot eyes, and breathed heavily. "Why the fuck have you been ignorin' my calls?"

Deluxe looked at his uncle, who still had on the blood stained outfit, and wondered what happened, but didn't bother to ask. "Look, I told you that night at the casino I was finished. I ain't fuckin' wit you like that no more."

Gator couldn't believe what he was hearing. After all he'd done for Deluxe, Gator couldn't believe that his ungrateful nephew was leaving him at a time like this. For the first time since getting in the game, he was really on his own.

"Nigga, after all I did for you, this is how you fuckin' repay me?" Gator screamed.

Seeing that his uncle looked high, Deluxe told him, "Unc go the fuck on wit' that shit. You high and I got my own shit to worry about. I ran into Myth and some shit got real hot in the streets."

"Yeah, I heard he almost bodied yo' ass," Gator replied sarcastically. "When you plan on gettin' his ass back? Do you know that nigga had the nerve to take over one of my dope houses?"

"Don't worry about that. I'll take care of Myth, but just understand, I ain't doin' it for you. That muthafucka almost killed me and my girl so he really gotta go now."

Gator was shocked at what he was hearing. "So, let me get this shit straight. You can finally get off yo' ass and put a end to that nigga for some hoe, but you can't do shit for yo' fam? And since when did she become yo' girl?"

"Don't call her a hoe."

"And why not. She still fuckin' for money right? Why do you always fall in love wit' everybody you fuck? You soft-ass nigga," Gator teased. "As a matter of fact, do you really wanna know who she is?"

"No, I don't."

"Speaking of the hoe, where is she now? Y'all better not be fuckin' in my mother's bed."

"She's at home, but you need to worry about…" Deluxe knew that he wasn't going to get anywhere with his uncle, especially while he was high. "Like I said, I'ma handle Myth's bitch-ass, just don't get it twisted and think that I'm doin' it for you," he said, heading upstairs.

Yeah Myth won't be the only bitch-ass to get dealt wit' either. I know exactly how to get yo' ass back now, Gator thought to himself, as he watched Deluxe turn his back on him.

His rage grew deeper as thoughts of his nephew going all out for a bitch who turned tricks at the casino, but not for his family. Gator shook his head in disgust as he plotted what his next move was going to be.

He needed to find someone else that he could manipulate

and he knew just the person to get on his team. Gator looked at his watch to see what the time was, and after realizing that it was almost nine he knew exactly where to go to find his mark. He walked back upstairs, without saying another word to his nephew and headed out the door. Finally looking at the bullet holes in Deluxe's truck, he shook his head and thought, *Myth shoulda killed you and that bitch.*

● ●

Still coked up and high as a kite, Gator left Momma Ruth's house and headed straight for the casino. *That bitch ain't at home. Once a hoe, always a hoe,* he thought as he stepped on the gas. It didn't take Gator long to reach the casino from his mother's house. After pulling up to the valet stand, he made sure to grab a bag from the backseat before exiting the car. When the valet attendant gave him a parking ticket, he quickly made his way inside the casino.

He figured he would find the trick's where they always were, working the high rollers area. Walking through the casino toward the crap tables, Gator finally saw exactly who he was looking for. Like he figured, she was working the floor wearing a black dress that hugged every curve of her fat ass. Every move that she made mesmerized him as he thought about ripping her dress off and plowing his dick deep into her wet pussy. Licking his lips at the thought of her pussy dripping over his face, his dick began to do a dance in the boxer briefs he wore.

Sensing that someone was watching her, Yasmin turned around to find Gator staring at her with a possessed look in his eyes. Not wanting to draw any bad attention to them, she smiled and gave him a look that said, get the fuck outta here. Ignoring Yasmin's offensive gaze, Gator motioned for her to come to him.

Immediately, she could tell that something was wrong. To avoid causing a scene, she whispered something in the ear of the man who she was working on, and walked over to where Gator stood.

Talking quietly so that no one around them could hear, Yasmin firmly asked, "What the fuck are you doing here? Is something wrong with Deluxe?"

"Now, is that anyway to greet yo' man?" Gator asked, as he pulled her closer to him.

"First of all, you ain't my muthafuckin' man. I gotta a man, a real man, your fine ass nephew remember!"

"Fuck that nigga. You got his dumb-ass thinkin' that you at home, when you over this muthafucka trickin' as usual. That's why his ass almost got you killed."

Yasmin was heated. "Listen, I don't have time for this bull-shit. What do you want?"

"Besides fuckin' you?" Gator replied, as he smacked Yasmin on the ass. "We both got a problem that I think we can solve together!"

Confused by what Gator was talking about, Yasmin replied, "Problem...I ain't got no problems, other than you fucking up my money right now."

"Bitch, I got money, now lets go upstairs so we can be alone."

Yasmin laughed. "Oh, really. Well that ain't what I heard. Now leave me alone so I can finish workin' these *real* paid men up in here." She started to walk away until Gator grabbed her arm.

Gator looked at Yasmin like he could smack the shit out of her as he sucked his teeth. "Look, I know who killed your father!"

CHAPTER 22

Yasmin couldn't believe what she'd just heard. Stopping in her tracks, she spun around and looked at Gator with a confused look. "What did you just say?"

Seeing that he'd finally gotten her attention, Gator smiled. "You heard me. I know who killed your father. Detective Hughes." He could tell that those words sunk deep into her heart. Her feisty attitude had quickly been transformed. "Now, like I said earlier, let's go upstairs so we can talk. I know yo' ass got a room!"

"No, actually I don't. My tricks normally get them."

"Well, if you wanna know what happened to yo' pops, you need to get one," Gator replied. "Oh, and by the way you payin'."

A part of her thought Gator was lying just to get her upstairs, but Yasmin had to at least find out if he was telling the truth. She desperately wanted to know who'd killed her father and why, so this was the prime opportunity to get some answers.

Ten minutes later, Yasmin and Gator walked inside the plush hotel room. Gator threw the bag he was carrying onto the bed then made his way straight to the mini-bar to keep his high going. He grabbed two small bottles of Ciroc that were displayed, and gulped each one down in a matter of seconds. Looking around the room, he walked over to the huge California king-sized bed and plopped his body down on top of it.

Seeing that Gator was taking his precious time about telling her who'd supposedly killed her father, Yasmin started getting impatient. "So, who the fuck killed my father?"

Licking his lips, Gator replied, "First things first, come over here and give daddy some head."

Disgusted at the thought of sucking Gator's dick, Yasmin stood by the bar with her arms folded. "I didn't come up here for this shit. Are you gonna tell me or not!"

"Bitch, I just told you, dick before information." He quickly untied the belt to his linen pants. "Now get the fuck over here!"

Realizing that there was no other way around the situation, Yasmin lowered her head as she walked over to the bed. Laughing to himself, Gator sat on the edge of the bed stroking his dick as he watched Yasmin's ass swing from side to side.

Wanting to get the whole ordeal over with, Yasmin knelt down and grabbed Gator's dick with her hands and began to stroke it up and down. She didn't want to put his dick anywhere near her mouth, so she figured if she jacked him off for a while, she wouldn't have to suck it that long. Gator laid back on the bed and began to moan with every stroke that Yasmin made. Seeing that his dick was starting to throb, Yasmin lowered her thick lips onto the head then began to deep throat him in hopes that it would make him cum quick.

Her warm wet mouth made Gator imagine how good her pussy would be. This was the first time since Mylani had been killed that he was actually getting his dick sucked, and it felt wonderful. Gator grabbed the back of Yasmin's head as she picked up the pace and began to hump her face. The force that he applied caused her to gag and spit on his dick, which then made Gator hump faster and harder. Sensing that he was about to cum, Yasmin took his manhood out her mouth and stroked it in her hand hard and fast.

Screaming, "Faster bitch! Faster," Gator let out a loud moan as he finally shot his load of cum all over Yasmin's hands.

Relieved that the whole ordeal was over, Yasmin got up and went into the bathroom to wash her hands and gargle. She couldn't wait to get the taste of his disgusting dick out of her mouth. Meanwhile, as she cleaned herself up, Gator couldn't stop smiling.

Like I said, once a hoe always a hoe. We'll see what my punk-ass nephew thinks when he finds out I bust a nut over his so called girls face, he thought sitting up. After pulling his pants back up, Yasmin returned from the bathroom, and looked at Gator with complete hatred.

"I can't believe you made me do that shit first," she said in disbelief.

Gator continued to smile, which almost made Yasmin's stomach turn. "Are you just mad 'cause you didn't get paid for yo' services, hoe? In that case, here." Gator pulled out a five dollar bill, which was some of the change from the airport parking, and handed it to Yasmin. "That should be enough."

"Fuck you. Now, who killed my father?"

"Your precious Deluxe did," Gator replied bluntly.

Those words hit Yasmin like a ton of bricks. She couldn't believe what she was hearing, and none of it was making sense. She was confused and needed answers.

"Why the fuck would you say something like that?" Yasmin screamed. "I don't believe you. You're fucking lying!"

Knowing that Yasmin might not believe him, Gator reached over, grabbed the bag and pulled out something he knew would get her attention. "You probably don't remember, but they never found yo' father's citation holder," he said, handing Yasmin the black vinyl book. "Well, the reason why they never found it is because Deluxe took it after he murdered him."

Yasmin's eyes began to well up with water as she opened

up the book and saw her father's name and badge number inscribed on the inside. *Detective Jerome Hughes, Detroit Narcotics Task Force #42801.* She couldn't believe that Deluxe was the one responsible for killing her father. Yasmin continued to slowly flip through the citation book as her face became drowned in tears. Seeing that this was his chance to get Deluxe back, Gator walked over to Yasmin and lifted her head up.

He went on to describe the scene of the murder on that night, and gave Yasmin the complete details, which proved he had to be telling the truth. "Listen, that piece of shit nephew of mine is a foul muthafucka. He crossed me too. For all I know he had somethin' to do wit' my fiancé being killed." Wiping the tears from her face, Gator continued, "We need to make him pay for what he's done, and you the only one who can help me do it. He's out of control and his ass can't be trusted!"

Yasmin knew that Gator was shady and couldn't be trusted either, but she also couldn't come to grips that Deluxe was the cold blooded killer who'd killed her father and possibly Gator's fiancé. Unable to talk, Yasmin finally nodded her head up and down in agreement with Gator's plan to make Deluxe pay for what he did.

• •

It had been a couple of days since Gator showed up at Momma Ruth's house declaring war on Deluxe. With Gator back in town, Deluxe knew it was only a matter of time before things would get hotter than they already were in the streets. He knew that he had to find Myth and put a few slugs in his head before it was too late. Ever since the shoot out at the beauty salon, Deluxe was even more convinced that he needed to get out of the game, and now he finally had someone who was worth getting out of the game for. He wasn't going to let Gator or Myth fuck that up for him.

For hours, Deluxe had been all over the west side looking for Myth. He figured with Myth now running shit he would be able to find him at one of his corners making sure things were being handled right. However, everywhere he went there was no sign of the big man. That's when it hit him. Today was Myth's son's birthday. Deluxe had been hearing the advertisement about a big party on the radio all week, and in true big dog fashion, he knew Myth would be going all out for his son. If it was anytime to catch him slipping, this was it. The party was being held at Asbury Park, and hosted by The Bushman from WJLB. Everyone in the city was expected to come and show the new boss of the city some love. However, the one person who wasn't expected to accept the public invitation was Deluxe.

Since becoming Jimmy's right hand man, Myth's arrogance had grown big time. He wanted to do everything bigger and better than Gator. Even though Jimmy hated flashy associates, he allowed Myth to carry on in that manner as a way to taunt Gator. Jimmy knew that Gator was broke and powerless, and it was only a matter of time before Gator would be dead and out of the way permanently. Although Myth had come close to kissing the warm lips of the hot slugs that Deluxe had express mailed to him, he was beginning to feel like he was unstoppable. He had filled Gator's shoes in no time.

Deluxe crept up Grand River toward Asbury Park where the party was in full swing. As he approached the park, he could see rows of cars lined up. He continued up the street toward Fenkell, and looked for Myth's Lexus, but surprisingly didn't see it. Figuring that Myth hadn't showed up yet, he decided to post up and wait like the trained sniper he was, rather than risk being spotted by circling the block.

Twenty minutes passed before Deluxe finally noticed Myth's LS creeping up the street. He slid down in the seat slightly so Myth wouldn't spot him, then desperately hoped the bullet hole truck wouldn't be noticed as well. As Myth drove by, Deluxe could barely see inside because of all the smoke that clouded the windows.

"Good, that nigga is gettin' fucked up as usual, so he probably didn't see me," Deluxe said, as he watched his enemy park a few spaces up the block. The smoke was also a clear indication that his son wasn't in the car as well, making things even better for Deluxe. He wasn't one to kill in front of children. Trying to catch Myth before he got out the car, Deluxe pulled out his gun, then slowly slid out the truck. Looking around, he quietly crept up to the passenger side door of the Lexus then opened it with full force. After jumping inside, his Glock was shoved into the side of Myth's face within seconds.

Myth dropped the blunt that was hanging from his mouth causing him to jump. "Aah shit, what the fuck!" he screamed, instantly putting his hands in the air.

"Put yo' muthafuckin' hands down nigga. You know this ain't no fuckin' stick up," Deluxe replied through his gritted teeth.

"Waaait, waaait, waaait a minute, Deluxe. I can use someone like you on my team baby," Myth said, in a shaky voice.

"Nigga I ain't tryin' to work for you. I'm done wit' all this bullshit."

"Please don't do this in front of my son's party!" Myth begged.

"Nigga, you tried to kill me and my girl and now you bitchin' up, fuck you!" Deluxe cocked his gun.

Still trying to cop a plea for his life, Myth whispered, "Hold on, hold on. I got some information for you that you need to hear first."

"Man, I don't need to hear shit."

"I think you do. You need to know who killed yo' pops."

Caught off guard, Deluxe questioned, "My pops? What the fuck you talkin' about nigga? You just sayin' shit, to buy time."

"Deluxe, I'm serious. I know what happened to Rock the night he was killed. It wasn't no drug deal gone bad like Gator said. He was set up!"

"Look nigga, I'ma kill you then that fuckin' son of yours if you keep fuckin' wit' me."

"I swear on my son's life, I know who killed yo' pops!"

Not sure whether he should believe him, Deluxe pulled out a pair of handcuffs and cuffed Myth's hands to the steering wheel. Lowering the gun from Myth's face he said, "Nigga you got five seconds to tell me what the fuck you talkin' about."

Myth immediately went into detail about the night Rock was killed. He told Deluxe everything that happened and everyone who was there, but failed to say who'd actually pulled the trigger. Growing impatient, Deluxe told Myth that he was tired of him stalling, and that his time was up. As Deluxe lifted his gun toward the side of Myth's head, he screamed, "It was Gator. Gator killed Rock!"

CHAPTER 23

Deluxe couldn't believe what Myth had just told him. He knew that Gator was one of the shadiest niggas he knew, but he just couldn't believe that his uncle would actually stoop that low. Myth went on to tell Deluxe where everything happened and how it all went down.

"Why? Why did he kill him?" Deluxe asked.

"It's simple…jealously. He hated everything about Rock. Shit, he even hates you."

Still in shock and disbelief, Deluxe clenched his jaw then lowered his gun one final time. Not sure what to make of his reaction, Myth sat quietly in the car hoping that Deluxe wouldn't go postal. Seconds later, and without anymore said, Deluxe opened the car door and got out. Thinking it was all a set up and that he would come back, Myth looked in his rearview mirror, and watched as Deluxe walked in the opposite direction. It wasn't until he saw Deluxe climb into the Escalade and peel off down the street that he knew his life had been spared for the time being. His plan couldn't have worked out any better. Myth knew that Deluxe would turn his attention to Gator and get rid of his former friend once at for all. A task that he wouldn't have to do.

Driving down the street like a mad man, Deluxe needed someone to talk to quickly before he did something crazy like drive off a bridge. Knowing there was only one person in his life that he could trust, Deluxe whipped out his phone and called Yasmin. It had been a couple of days since he'd seen or even spoken to her, and now he needed his girl more than ever.

"What's up baby? I haven't heard from you in a few days. I thought you quit loving me," the soft sweet voice on the other end of the phone said.

"I need to see you. I got some shit on my mind," Deluxe responded, almost breaking down in tears.

"What's wrong? Are you alright?"

"No, not at all. I'm all fucked up right now," he replied, in a solemn voice. "I just found out some foul shit about my father."

"Well, I'm at home, so come over. No one's here."

"I'm on my way."

The ride over to Yasmin's aunt's house was a long one for Deluxe. He replayed the conversation that he had had with Myth over and over in his head. *This muthafucka has been preachin' about loyalty to me since day one and he fuckin' killed my pops,* Deluxe thought as he continued to drive. All of his life he wanted to find out what happened to his father, and never in a million years, would he have thought Gator was the one responsible. The news was devastating.

When Deluxe pulled up in front of Yasmin's house, he sat in the car for a few minutes to get himself together before going inside. He wiped the tears that had finally fallen down his cheek and hopped out of the car. However, before he could even make it to the house, Yasmin opened the front door, ran outside and met him with a hug. Feeling safe in her arms, Deluxe held her tight and began to cry all over again. This was the first time since they'd been messing with each other that Yasmin had ever seen this side of him.

After a long embrace, she walked Deluxe into the house, then sat down with him on the couch as he laid his head on her shoulders.

"What's wrong? I've never seen you like this. Talk to me," Yasmin pleaded, as she kissed Deluxe on the cheek. She deserved an award for the way she carried on because little did Deluxe know she wanted to shoot him at point blank range. Yasmin had plans for Deluxe, but it wasn't time.

"I'm sorry baby girl. I never wanted you to see me like this."

"It's okay. We all have to cry sometimes."

Smiling at Yasmin's beautiful face, Deluxe took a deep breath and told her how he'd ran into the guy who tried to kill them that day, and how he'd told him what really happened to his father.

With a puzzled look on her face, Yasmin asked, "I'm confused. What happened with your father, and why would the guy who you had the shootout with tell you something like that."

"It's a long story, but the short version is that my uncle Gator killed my father...in cold blood. He took my father away from me."

Yasmin was shocked. Thoughts about Gator and his shady intentions instantly started floating around in her head. *Maybe that asshole was lying to me about Deluxe. Maybe he was the one who really killed my dad. Maybe he's just trying to use me to get what he wants.*

She knew all too well the way he felt, and gave Deluxe another hug. "Baby, I understand. I know what it's like to have your father taken from you. My father was murdered because someone decided that his life wasn't worth anything either."

Yasmin had never gone into details about what happened to her father, and felt this was the perfect opportunity to express her feelings. She lifted Deluxe's head and kissed his lips, bringing a slight smile to his face.

"Everyday I think about my father and what happened to

him. I know exactly how you're feeling right now. I promised my-self that if I ever found out who killed him that I would go after them myself. I think you should do the same," Yasmin confided. "I know he's your uncle, but he has to go."

Even though he'd already made that decision, Deluxe was surprised to hear Yasmin's suggestion. But she was right. Gator had to pay for everything he'd done. Deluxe didn't even bother to mention that while he'd been staying at Momma Ruth's house and collecting the mail her autopsy report finally came. As it turned out, Momma Ruth's cause of death was from a single gun shot wound to her chest by a 9mm bullet. Deluxe had a .40 caliber that day, and clearly remembered Sonny having a .38, so in actuality she'd been killed by her own son.

"Did you hear what I said?" Yasmin asked, rubbing Deluxe's hand. "Your uncle is conniving and evil and deserves to die for all the shit he did to you and your family. He's done every-thing in his power to try and make you a monster like him," she continued, as Deluxe thought about how he was going to end his uncle's life.

Yasmin told Deluxe that she would help him set Gator up. All he had to do was say the word. Thinking about her offer and looking at the sincerity in her eyes, Deluxe agreed to let Yasmin help him get rid of his uncle.

"I know you would do it for me if you knew who killed my father," Yasmin said, as the two sealed the deal with a hug and a deep kiss.

CHAPTER 24

Deluxe and Yasmin spent the next couple of days coming up with how they were going to send Gator on a first class trip to hell. On the other hand, she'd been avoiding Gator's phone calls. While she focused on Deluxe and his needs, Gator was becoming impatient by the minute. He needed Yasmin to help him get to Deluxe, and knew the task couldn't be done without her.

Growing tired of hearing her phone ring almost every second, and Deluxe always asking who it was, Yasmin finally answered.

"Where the fuck you been girl?" Gator yelled as soon as he heard her voice. "I been tryin' to reach yo' ass for days now."

"Oh sorry. I've been tryin' to take care of some business."

"Well, what up? When we gonna get that nigga?"

"Look, lets not talk about this over the phone. Where can we meet?"

"Meet me at my office on the east side," Gator replied excitedly. "Let's get this shit poppin."

Before ending the call, Gator made sure to give Yasmin the

address, then told her that he couldn't wait to see the look on his nephew's face once he found out she was on his team. After hanging up with Gator, Yasmin called Deluxe and told him that she was supposed to meet with his uncle in an hour, and where the location was. They talked for a few short minutes before Deluxe thanked Yasmin for helping him out, then prepared to get himself together for what was about to take place. He'd waited for years to be face to face with his father's killer, and tonight it was all about to go down.

Deluxe jumped in the shower at the hotel he'd been staying in, and thought about how the uncle he loved so much was responsible for taking away everyone he ever loved. He told Yasmin that they needed to leave town after tonight because he no longer wanted their safety to be in jeopardy. Besides, if something ever happened to her, Deluxe didn't know what he would do. Leaving town would give them a chance to start a new life together. They both had been talking about getting out of the game, and now it was time for them to act on it. Even if it meant he had to be a father to her two sisters, Deluxe was willing to do whatever it took.

Being conscious of the time, he jumped out of the shower and got dressed. Deluxe expected Gator to try and get to the meeting spot a few minutes early, so he wanted to beat him there. Looking at a picture of his grandmother on the small nightstand, Deluxe kissed it before he left and said that he was finally going to make this right for her, Mylani, and his father. After putting on his shoes, Deluxe grabbed his bulletproof vest, his gun, and shot out the door.

It didn't take long for Deluxe to get to Gator's office from his hotel. Just like he told Yasmin he would do, Deluxe parked his car two blocks away so that Gator wouldn't see it, nor suspect anything. Once he looked at the clock and realized it was 9:45 p.m. he figured that Yasmin and Gator would be arriving soon, so he needed to make his move.

Using the key, Gator had given to him a long time ago, Deluxe waited inside Gator's conference room for both of them to show up. The fifteen minutes that he'd been waiting felt like an eternity to him. He'd been on plenty of scouting missions in the Marines, but none of them had the implications that this one had. He was finally going to look into the eyes of the man who killed his father.

At ten o'clock on the dot, Deluxe heard both Gator and Yasmin pulling into the parking lot. His palms began to sweat as he anticipated seeing the look in his uncle's eyes when he opened up the conference room door. Deluxe sat patiently at the head of the table, in his all black hoodie and vest. He even wore black leather gloves as he gripped the pistol tight in his right hand.

"It's 'bout time. You ready to do this?" Gator asked as he

and Yasmin walked into his office.

"Yep, I've been waiting for this day for a long time," Yasmin replied.

"I can't wait to body that…" Gator stopped in mid sentence when he opened the door and turned on the light to the conference room. He was absolutely stunned when he saw Deluxe sitting at the table with a gun pointed directly at his forehead.

"You fuckin' bitch. Yo' ass set me up!" Gator screamed in Yasmin's direction. "I don't know why I trusted yo' ass."

"Shut the fuck up!" Deluxe responded, as Yasmin quickly got out the way. He was tired of hearing his uncle's mouth for once. "Tell me why. Just fuckin' tell me why?"

"Why what?" Gator asked with no emotion. For some strange reason he knew where the conversation was headed.

Fighting back his emotions, Deluxe replied, "Myth told me what really happened to my father. You killed him!"

Strangely, Gator began to laugh hysterically. "And you believed that shit."

Deluxe was beyond furious. "What the hell are you talkin' about? Why wouldn't I believe him? He told me everything. You shot my father in broad fuckin' daylight. How could you kill your own damn brother?"

Yasmin continued to watch as the two men eyed each other

like pit bulls.

"Deluxe, Deluxe Deluxe…I didn't kill your father. Myth did."

Now, more confused than ever, Deluxe began to shake his head back and forth. "Stop lying you piece of shit. You shot him. I know you did. It was even a bullet from your fuckin' gun that killed Momma Ruth too."

Gator still held a devilish grin. "I'm not lying. Technically, Myth killed Rock because he was the muthafucka who pulled the trigger. I just sat back and watched."

Deluxe felt sick, and at this point really didn't know who to believe. However, a part of him wished he'd killed Myth while he had the chance.

"You think I give a fuck about what happened to my mother, or yo' punk-ass daddy?" Gator begin to yell. "That bitch worshipped the ground that nigga walked on. I shoulda killed her ass a long time ago," he remarked, sending shockwaves through Deluxe' body. "Rock sold drugs and did dirt just like me, but everybody put his bitch-ass up on a pedestal and treated me like shit. Hell yeah, I watched his ass die. Just like I wanna sit here and watch you die!"

Deluxe couldn't believe what he was hearing. With every word that Gator spat, Deluxe grew more and more numb. Every ounce of love that he once had for his uncle was completely gone.

He never imagined that his own flesh and blood could be so cruel.

"You think I'm scared of dying nigga?" Gator continued.

Fuck yo…"

Before Gator could get the rest of his sentence out, Deluxe

pulled the trigger, sending Gator to hell with a hollow tip between

his eyes. Still overcome with rage and hurt, Deluxe stood over his

uncle's lifeless body and continued to squeeze the trigger until

nothing was left. After all the years of being his uncle's puppet,

Deluxe was finally able to get the revenge that he'd hoped for. He

was finally out of the game and able to live a normal life. No more

drugs, no more killing, and no more searching for his father's

killer. It was finally over.

EPILOUGE

Deluxe poured two glasses of Dom Perignon, then sat each glass on top of the cherry wood nightstand. Sitting on the plush king sized bed, he looked around the master bedroom of the private villa, and smiled. It was perfect. He and Yasmin had only been in Cabo San Lucas for two hours, and he'd fallen in love with the place already. Finally using the plane ticket Gator had given to him a few weeks ago, Deluxe planned on enjoying every minute of the two week vacation with his new fiancé. After agreeing to put her high class hoeing days behind, Deluxe got on one knee and presented Yasmin with a platinum two carat engagement ring. A part of him knew it was a little too soon to be getting married to someone he barely knew, but he decided to take a chance anyway. Besides, Yasmin was his only family now.

Deluxe smiled again when he thought about his old street 'fam'. A family that started out with four and now there was none. He'd heard that after word got around about Gator being killed, Myth got even cockier around town, and officially declared himself as the new street king. However, the notoriety didn't last long.

He was arrested soon after when cops raided one of his west side dope houses. Even Jimmy the Greek had decided to skip town. Deluxe was more than happy that the negative part of his life was over. All he wanted to do now was start over, and concentrate on the beautiful new woman he'd planned to marry.

Deluxe lit a few scented the candles and placed them throughout the room as he waited for Yasmin to get out of the shower. Hearing the water turn off a few seconds later, Deluxe sat on the bed, fully dressed and anxiously waited to see her gorgeous model-like body.

When the bathroom door finally opened, he wasn't disappointed.

Damn she fine as a muthafucka, Deluxe thought as Yasmin seductively walked toward him dripping wet. The sunlight hit her caramel colored body in all the right places. As she got closer to the bed, Deluxe stood up as his dick began to throb. He stared at her body like a work of art.

Licking his lips, Deluxe got down on his knees and began to suck on Yasmin' pussy like it was his last meal. With every thrust of his tongue, Yasmin moaned and rocked her hips forcing him to take a mouth full of her. She loved the way Deluxe fucked her with his face. He continued to flick his tongue over her clit as he sucked up all her juices at the same time.

"That feels so fucking good. Don't stop, Daddy don't stop," Yasmin demanded as she rocked her hips harder and faster. "Oh shit. I'm about to cum. Don't stop, suck this pussy baby. Suck this pussy!" Yasmin screamed as she unloaded all of her juices on Deluxe' face.

Loving every minute, Deluxe continued to lick Yasmin until he had tasted every drop of her. From the start of their relationship, sex between the two of them had always been explosive, and it still was. Deluxe knew that after he would make her cum, he would be in for a long passionate night of fucking, and could barely wait.

"Was that good enough for you, baby girl?" Deluxe asked, finally coming up for air.

Still unable to get her thoughts together, Yasmin smiled and nodded. "Can you go get me a wash cloth, Daddy?" She rubbed the side of his face. "You got me all wet and nasty over here."

"I'll be happy to," Deluxe replied without hesitation. He stood up and walked toward the bathroom with a huge smile.

"And make sure you get it nice and hot with lots of soap baby," she yelled, in order to buy more time.

Looking back to make sure he was completely out of sight, Yasmin quickly sprung into action. She grabbed her handbag and pulled out a prescription type bottle before placing two small pills in one of the champagne glasses. Deluxe walked back into the room just as she was swirling both glasses around in her hand.

"What you doin'?" Deluxe asked, as he approached the bed.

"Just twirling our drinks around to release the flavor of the champagne. After you clean me up, I want to make a toast and finish what we started," she replied seductively. She placed the glasses back down, making sure she knew which one was tainted, then laid back on the bed. Opening her legs, she gave her man a full view of her treasure.

"A toast? What we toastin' to?" Deluxe asked, as he cleaned Yasmin's love area.

"To us."

"Oh, that's right. To the future Mrs. Green."

After wiping off the last spot, Yasmin smiled and handed Deluxe one of the champagne glasses. Wrapping their arms around each other, Yasmin whispered, "Till death do us part baby."

"Till death do us part," Deluxe replied, as he drank all the champagne that was in his glass.

She displayed a wicked smile before pushing him on the bed. "Take your clothes off."

Happy to see her taking charge, Deluxe happily obliged. However, by the time he got to his pants, he started feeling funny.

"Damn, I must've drunk that shit too fast. I'm startin' to feel a lil' light headed."

Yasmin knew that the pills were already starting to take effect. "Shhh. It's been a long day baby. Just lay back and let me take care of you."

Yasmin took a couple of ice cubes out of the bucket, and rubbed them on Deluxe's chest. Placing one of the cubes in her mouth, she grabbed his dick and began to lick it up and down. She then proceeded to take in all ten inches as he drifted further and further into a state of shock. With his dick still in her mouth, Yasmin reached inside the bucket and grabbed the ice pick.

Seeing that the pills were finally causing his body to go limp, Yasmin removed his shaft, then slid her body on top of his. "This is for my father, Detective Hughes."

Deluxe's eyes rolled to the back of his head. He wanted to open them wider, but couldn't.

Without saying another word, Yasmin grabbed the ice pick and shoved it violently into Deluxe's neck piercing his jugular vein in the process. He was dead within minutes.

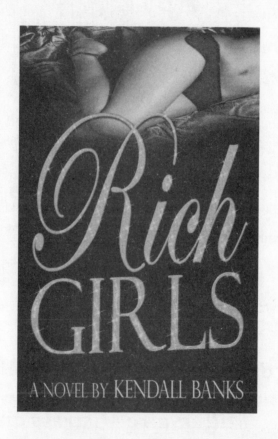

**A hot new novel
by Tiphani
Essence Magazine Bestselling
Author of
Millionaire Mistress and
Still A Mistress
Coming Nov '08**

ORDER FORM

MAIL TO:
PO Box 423
Brandywine, MD 20613
301-362-6508

FAX TO:
301-579-9913

Ship to:	
Address:	

City & State	Zip
Attention:	

Date:	
Phone	
E-mail	

Make all checks and money orders payable to **Life Changing Books**

Qty.	ISBN	Title	Release Date	Price
	0-9741394-0-8	A Life To Remember by Azarel	Aug-03	$ 15.00
	0-9741394-1-6	Double Life by Tyrone Wallace	Nov-04	$ 15.00
	0-9741394-5-9	Nothin Personal by Tyrone Wallace	Jul-06	$ 15.00
	0-9741394-2-4	Bruised by Azarel	Jul-05	$ 15.00
	0-9741394-7-5	Bruised 2: The Ultimate Revenge by Azarel	Oct-06	$ 15.00
	0-9741394-3-2	Secrets of a Housewife by J. Tremble	Feb-06	$ 15.00
	0-9724003-5-4	i Shoulda Seen It Comin by Danette Majette	Jan-06	$ 15.00
	0-9741394-4-0	The Take Over by Tonya Ridley	Apr-06	$ 15.00
	0-9741394-6-7	The Millionaire Mistress by Tiphani	Nov-06	$ 15.00
	1-934230-99-5	More Secrets More Lies by J. Tremble	Feb-07	$ 15.00
	1-934230-98-7	Young Assassin by Mike G	Mar-07	$ 15.00
	1-934230-95-2	A Private Affair by Mike Warren	May-07	$ 15.00
	1-934230-94-4	All That Glitters by Ericka M. Williams	Jul-07	$ 15.00
	1-934230-93-6	Deep by Danette Majette	Jul-07	$ 15.00
	1-934230-96-0	Flexin & Sexin by K'wan, Anna J & Others	Jun-07	$ 15.00
	1-934230-92-8	Talk of the Town by Tonya Ridley	Jul-07	$ 15.00
	1-934230-89-8	Still a Mistress by Tiphani	Nov-07	$ 15.00
	1-934230-91-X	Daddy's House by Azarel	Nov-07	$ 15.00
	1-934230-87-1-	Reign of a Hustler by Nissa A. Showell	Jan-08	$ 15.00
	1-934230-86-3	Something He Can Feel by Marissa Monteilh	Feb-08	$ 15.00
	1-934230-88-X	Naughty Little Angel by J. Tremble	Feb-08	$ 15.00
	1-934230847	In Those Jeans	Jun-08	$ 15.00
	1-934230855	Marked	Jul-08	$ 15.00
			Total for Books	$

Shipping Charges (add $4.25 for 1-4 books*)	$
Total Enclosed (add lines)	$

* **Prison Orders- Please allow up to three (3) weeks for delivery.**

For credit card orders and orders over 25 books, please contact us at orders@lifechaningbooks.net (Cheaper rates for COD orders)

*Shipping and Handling of 5-10 books is $6.25, please contact us if your order is more than 10 books. (301)362-6508